ABOUT THE AUTHOR

Christopher Pike was born in New York, but grew up in Los Angeles, where he lives to this day. Prior to becoming a writer he worked in a factory, painted houses and programmed computers. His hobbies include astronomy, meditating, running, and making sure his books are prominently displayed in his local bookshop. As well as being a bestselling children's writer, he is also the author of three books for adults.

Spooksville

Spooksville

ALIENS IN THE SKY

Christopher Pike

**Hodder
Children's
Books**

a division of Hodder Headline plc

First published in the USA in 1996
by Pocket Books

First published in Great Britain in 1996
by Hodder Children's Books

10 9 8 7 6

A Catalogue record for this book is available from the British Library

ISBN 0-340-66116-X

Typeset by Avon Dataset Ltd, Bidford-on-Avon, Warks.

Printed and bound in Great Britain by
Cox & Wyman Ltd, Reading, Berks.

Hodder Children's Books
a division of Hodder Headline plc
338 Euston Road
London NW1 3BH

One

Spooksville seldom got real hot. Nestled between the hills beside the ocean, there was usually a cool breeze around the corner to prevent it from becoming uncomfortable, even in the middle of summer. But in the last half of July, only a couple of weeks after Adam and his friends had got trapped in the Haunted Cave, the temperature rose sharply. At midday, the thermometer burst past a hundred degrees. To get away from the heat, Sally suggested they head up to the reservoir.

'We won't go in the water,' she said. 'You don't want to do that. But it's always cooler up there.'

The four of them: Sally, Adam, Watch and Cindy were seated on Cindy's porch, drinking sodas and wiping their sweat-soaked brows. Adam stared at the half burnt-down lighthouse – about half a kilometre away – where earlier in the summer he had wrestled with a ghost. He felt like he was about to catch fire. He couldn't remember it ever having been so hot in Kansas City, which was known for its hot summers. He wondered what had brought the heat.

'Why can't you go in the water?' Cindy asked.

'Because you'll die,' Sally said simply.

'There are no fish in the reservoir,' Watch added. 'There's something unhealthy about the water.'

'But Spooksville gets its water from the reservoir,' Adam said.

'That's why so many children in town are born with deformities,' Sally said.

Cindy smiled. 'You were born here, Sally. That explains so much.'

'Not all deformities are bad,' Sally replied.

'The water is filtered before we drink it,' Watch said.

'What's filtered out?' Adam asked.

'I don't know,' Watch said. 'But it must be toxic stuff. The filtration plant has a habit of blowing up every couple of years.'

'Why is it cooler at the reservoir?' Adam asked.

Sally spoke. 'It's because Madeline Templeton – the witch who founded this city two hundred years ago – tortured fifty innocent people to death up there. The horror of that event reverberates psychically to this day, making the whole area cold as ice.'

2

Cindy made a face. 'And you want to go there to cool off?'

Sally shrugged. 'There is horror on almost any street in Spooksville, if you look deep enough into the past. Why, on this exact spot, where your house was built, Madeline Templeton once cut off a kid's head and fastened it on to a goat.'

'Yuck!' Cindy said. 'That's gross.'

'Yeah, but the kid was supposed to look like a goat anyway,' Watch said.

'Yeah,' Sally agreed. 'Maybe the witch did him a favour.'

'I don't know if she tortured the people to death at the reservoir,' Watch continued. 'I heard that she just made them go swimming in the water, and their skin turned grey and their hair all fell out.'

'I would rather die than lose my beautiful hair,' Sally said, brushing her brunette locks aside.

'I think the area is cooler because of all the subterranean streams that run under the ground,' Watch said, finally answering Adam's question. 'If you put your ear to the ground, you definitely hear gurgling water.'

Adam wiped away more sweat. 'Well, should we go there?'

Cindy was doubtful. 'The Haunted Cave is up there.'

'The Haunted Cave can't hurt you unless you're stupid

enough to go inside it,' Sally said.

'Thank you, Sally, for so gently reminding me of a past mistake,' Cindy said.

Sally spoke sweetly. 'Don't mention it, Cindy.'

'The Haunted Cave is located on a hill above the reservoir,' Watch said. 'We couldn't ride our bikes there last time, but if we're not climbing any rocky hills we can take them. We can get there in less than twenty minutes.' He tugged at his T-shirt, trying to cool off. 'I wouldn't mind hanging out there until it gets dark.'

'What do you think is causing this heat?' Adam asked.

'Could be an inversion layer,' Watch said.

'Or a curse from Ann Templeton,' Sally said. 'Madeline Templeton's seductive and evil descendant. She likes the heat. She likes all us kids to suffer in it.'

Adam shrugged. 'I'm for going.' He glanced at Cindy. 'If it's all right with you.'

Sally leant over and spoke in a *loud* whisper in Watch's ear. 'Notice how our dear Adam doesn't make a move without checking with his sweet Cindy.'

Cindy glared at Sally. 'He's just being polite. That's spelled P . . . O . . . L . . . I . . . T . . . E. Look it up in the dictionary. I know you've never heard of the word.' Cindy spoke to Adam. 'My mother doesn't care what I do, as long as I'm home before sunset.'

4

'My mother doesn't care what I do as long as I don't die,' Sally muttered.

Adam stood up. 'Then it's decided. We'll ride up there and stay until sunset.'

The others also stood up. Sally, as usual, wanted to have the last word.

'Let's leave before sunset,' she said. 'You never know what darkness might bring.'

Two

The bicycle ride up to the reservoir was harder than Adam had imagined. Because the place was in the hills behind Spooksville, they had to pedal on an incline most of the way. But it was the temperature that really stole Adam's strength. He was feeling wobbly when they arrived at the water and climbed off their bikes. Fortunately, they had each brought large plastic bottles of water.

'I feel a lot cooler now,' Adam said, sarcastically, as he opened his bottle and held it up to his lips. 'Now that we're here.'

'It's like being in an air-conditioned mall,' Cindy agreed, also reaching for her water bottle. Her face was red from the sun and the exertion.

'It actually is cooler here,' Watch said, stepping to the edge of the reservoir, which was a rough oval, maybe half a kilometre long, half that in width. The water was a strange grey colour. The surrounding bank was almost entirely devoid of trees. Their words seemed to die in the air the instant they left their mouths. Watch continued, 'It's got to be at least ten degrees cooler.'

'I feel refreshed from our ride,' Sally said, although she had already plopped down on a boulder and drained half her water bottle. 'I think my suggestion was a good one.'

Cindy had brought a bag of sandwiches. Finding shade beneath one of the few trees, they sat down and ate their food. As they munched and talked and drank, Adam did begin to feel a lot cooler. They had set off for the reservoir after four. It was now half past five, and the sun was just beginning to ease up on them. But it was still too hot to do much exploring, not that any of them were in the mood to try another local cave.

Watch happened to have a pack of cards on him, and wanted to play poker. Apparently Watch and Sally often played together. Adam was curious although he had never played the game before and didn't know the rules. But Cindy was uneasy.

'My mother doesn't approve of gambling,' Cindy said. 'She says it's immoral and disgusting.'

'Those two words fit me nicely,' Sally said jokingly. 'Listen, we're just going to gamble with smooth pebbles. We start with twenty each. It's not real gambling unless you have real money at stake. I mean, how can your mother be upset if you lose a pile of rocks?'

Cindy chuckled. 'You have a point there. All right, I will play as long as I don't have to wager my next week's allowance.'

Watch explained the rules of five card stud and for the next hour they played many hands. But Watch and Sally were way ahead of Adam and Cindy when it came to the subtleties of the game. Adam and Cindy quickly lost all their pebbles, and even fierce Sally was steadily withering under Watch's apparent skill. She got down to five pebbles, but finally seemed to be holding a strong hand because she bet two of them at once. Watch was unmoved; he matched her bet.

'I think you're bluffing,' he said confidently.

Sally caught his eye. 'You think so, babe.' She picked up the remainder of her pebbles. 'I raise you another three. Count them – seven grand on the table at once.'

Watch was unimpressed. 'I still think you're bluffing.'

Sally sneered. 'Thoughts aren't rocks. Put your pebbles where your mouth is.'

Coolly Watch matched her bet. 'There's ten grand on the table now.'

Sally was momentarily taken back. 'I can't believe you did that.'

'What have you got?' Watch asked.

Sally threw her cards down. 'Trash. You win. Darn.'

'It was an impressive bluff,' Adam told Sally.

'I fell for it,' Cindy agreed.

'It's not impressive unless it works,' Sally muttered.

The sun was getting near the horizon and they were thinking of returning home when a minor disaster struck. Cindy, who was still curious about the Haunted Cave, had hiked up to peek at the opening, just to see if it was closed or what. The others had allowed her to go by herself because she had promised not to step inside if it was open. She was on her way back down the hill, looking excited, when she must have stepped on some loose gravel. The ground seemed to go out from under her, and then she was toppling.

'Cindy!' Adam shouted. Sally and Watch looked over, and soon all three were running to Cindy's aid. In reality she had not toppled far, maybe five metres. But it was enough to pick up several scrapes and bruises. She was wearing shorts; her legs were bleeding slightly in a few places. But that was not the major problem. As they reached her, they saw her clutching her right ankle. Adam knelt by her side.

'Did you twist it?' he asked.

Cindy grimaced. 'Yeah. It hurts.'

'You didn't break it, did you?' Sally asked, concerned. 'Your bones are not sticking out, are they?'

'If you did break it, there's going to be no ambulance coming to your aid,' Watch said matter-of-factly. 'Spooksville's ambulance drivers have all long since disappeared.'

'Would you two shut up?' Adam said. 'Can't you see she's in pain?'

Cindy forced a smile. 'It's not too bad. I want to try putting some weight on it.'

'You might want to ice it first,' Watch suggested.

'Like we just happen to have bags of ice with us,' Sally said sarcastically.

Adam helped Cindy up. The moment Cindy put her right foot down, she let out a soft cry. 'Ah,' she said, breathing heavily. 'It really is sore.'

Adam pointed to the reservoir. 'Maybe you should soak it in the water. It will help with the swelling.'

'I wouldn't put my foot in that water if you'd just splashed sulphuric acid on my toes,' Sally said.

Watch strolled over to the water and crouched down. Before any of them could say a word, he reached over and cupped a handful of water. He raised it to his lips and swallowed, then nodded, satisfied.

'It could use a little fluoride, but otherwise it tastes fine,' he said.

'We should wait a minute and see if he falls over dead,' Sally whispered to Adam and Cindy.

Watch walked back to them. 'I don't think it will melt your skin off, Cindy. But put your whole foot in the water with your shoe still on. The pressure of the sides of the shoe will help the swelling as much as the cold water.'

'OK,' Cindy muttered, as Watch and Adam moved to either side and helped her to a spot where the water and ground met. She sat down, 'I feel like such a clutz, falling like that.'

'I fell,' Sally said proudly. 'Once. But I regained my balance before causing myself any harm.'

'Was the Haunted Cave open or closed?' Watch asked.

'It's still closed,' Cindy replied, as she carefully placed her aching ankle into the water. 'I didn't have the nerve to try to open it with one of the magic words we learned from the witch.' She twitched. 'Hey, this water is really cold.'

'Some people say the reservoir is bottomless,' Sally said. 'Certainly none of the bodies dumped here over the years have ever floated back to the surface.'

'I think I'm going to talk my parents into buying a water purifier when I get home,' Adam said. He clasped Cindy's hand and spoke in a gentle voice. 'Is the pain becoming less?'

'Oh, Watch,' Sally said, touching her heart. 'Look at his bedside manner. He's a born doctor. Dr Adam – he sounds like he could be a brain surgeon.'

'It feels better, thank you,' Cindy said, ignoring Sally. 'If I can just soak it for a few minutes, maybe I'll be able to ride back home.'

'You can ride a bike with one foot,' Sally said. 'Jaws does it all the time.'

'That's the kid who lost a leg to the great white shark who stays off our coast,' Watch reminded them.

'You're lucky there are no sharks in the reservoir,' Sally added.

'We'll wait here until you feel strong enough to travel,' Adam told Cindy.

Watch nodded toward the west. 'The sun is setting. It will be dark soon.'

'This is just what I was afraid would happen,' Sally said. She took a step away from the water and sat back down. 'There's no moon tonight. It will get black as ink up here.'

Three

Watch and Sally were both right. Not long after the sun left, the stars started to come out. As the night deepened, the numbers rose dramatically. Adam had never seen so many stars, nor had he ever enjoyed the Milky Way before. The faint nebulous river of the galaxy stretched across the entire sky. Watch, who seemed to know a great deal about astronomy, pointed out the Northern Cross and told them about the blue white star at the base of it.

'That's Deneb,' he said. 'It's tens of thousands of times brighter than our sun. I think it's the brightest star in the sky that we can see. It has a red star that circles it, but you can't see it with the naked eye.'

'But what about that one?' Sally asked, pointing straight overhead. 'That's several times brighter.'

'That's Vega,' Watch said. 'It's twenty-six light years away. It's also a lot brighter than our sun. But it's no

Deneb. Deneb is thousands of times further away than Vega. If Deneb was only twenty-six light years from here, it would dominate the whole sky.'

'How did you learn all these things?' Cindy asked, impressed.

In the dark, Watch shrugged. They could hardly see each other. Each of them was just a black line, drawn against the stars.

'I have a telescope at home,' Watch said. 'And I study the books on astronomy at the library. Mr Spiney has a few good ones.'

'Watch built his own telescope,' Sally said, with a trace of pride in her voice.

They were enjoying the stars, and listening to Watch's stories about the constellations so much, they hardly noticed the passage of time. Cindy had been soaking her foot for close to an hour when Adam suggested that she try putting weight on it again. They helped her up, and she gently put her foot down. She was about to tell them how it felt, but something remarkable interrupted her.

A strange light appeared in the sky.

'What the heck is that?' Sally gasped.

Straight overhead was a white light, much brighter than any star. At first it was just a point; they could not tell its size. But as they watched, it grew brighter, and they all

16

received the impression that it was coming towards them. Just then it stopped, hovering far above.

'Is it a plane?' Cindy whispered.

'A helicopter can hover,' Watch said. 'Not a plane. But I don't think it's a helicopter. We should be able to hear its rotary blades.'

'Could it be a balloon?' Adam asked.

'It's not moving like a balloon,' Watch said. 'It swept down and then just stopped.'

Sally chuckled uneasily. 'Well, it's not a flying saucer, is it?'

There was a moment of silence.

'That's exactly what I think it is,' Watch said finally.

'We should get out of here,' Cindy said.

'I don't know,' Adam said, getting excited. 'I've always wanted to see a UFO. Do you think it will land, Watch?'

Watch shrugged. 'This is Spooksville. Where else on Earth could an alien feel so at home?'

Perhaps the occupants aboard the strange light heard Watch. For at that moment it began to descend once more, dropping like a glowing meteorite out of a black abyss. They realised that they were staring at two vessels, not one. The ships had been flying so close together that their light had blurred. Adam's excitement was blunted by an edge of fear. The lights changed from white glows to

17

definite shapes. They were definitely flying saucers – and they were coming down fast.

They clearly intended to land at the reservoir.

'Maybe we should go hide behind the rocks,' Adam said quickly. 'At least at first.'

Watch considered for one second. 'Good idea. Can you walk, Cindy?'

'I can hobble if you guys help me,' she replied, fear in her voice. The saucers were now only half a kilometre overhead. Their brilliant white glow radiated out over the surface of the reservoir, turning it into one huge silver mirror. For a moment they halted again, apparently searching for a place to set down. Unfortunately the ships made up their minds swiftly.

The UFOs wanted to park beside their bikes.

'Let's carry her!' Adam shouted, as they stumbled slowly towards the large rocks, behind which they hoped to hide.

'Good idea!' Watch shouted back.

They didn't even ask Cindy for permission. They just each grabbed a leg and yanked her up so that she was riding above their shoulders. Sally ran ahead of them, leaping on to the rocks. She was clearly visible, they all were. Behind them, the saucers hovered five metres above their bicycles. Incredibly, there was no noise, not even a faint hum.

'I hope they didn't see us,' Adam gasped, as they carried

Cindy around the largest boulder and set her down. Above their heads, the glow stabbed past the edges of the rocks. Certain that Cindy was sitting comfortably, Adam, Sally and Watch climbed back up the boulders and peered over the edge.

Both ships had set down beside the water, practically on top of their bicycles. One continued to glow brilliantly. The other seemed to have turned off its engine or warp drive or whatever. It gave off a feeble white glow, nothing more. Both ships were saucer-shaped, circular, maybe ten metres in diameter. Actually, they looked like saucers with cups placed on top. It didn't take a genius to know they were not from planet Earth.

'What's happening?' Cindy whispered, below them.

'They're unloading an antimatter bomb and preparing to blow up the planet,' Sally said.

'Quiet,' Adam cautioned. 'They're just sitting there. Nothing's . . . Wait! I think I see a door opening.'

Adam was right. On the ship that was no longer glowing brightly, a door of sorts was materialising. It was a peculiar opening. There had been no sign of it a few seconds ago. It was as if the walls of the ship had suddenly dissolved in a rectangular pattern. Yellow light shone from inside. The door was not large; Adam would have had to stoop to enter the vessel.

19

'Do you see any aliens?' Adam asked.

'I'm the last person to ask,' Watch said. 'I'm half blind.'

'I hope they're not disgusting looking,' Sally whispered. 'Even E.T. gave me nightmares.'

'You can't think that way,' Watch said. 'They have probably travelled millions of miles to get here. They will have evolved from an entirely separate genetic tree. We will probably look horrible to them.'

'I think I look horrible to my own mother half the time,' Sally muttered.

'Shh,' Adam cautioned. 'One of them is coming out.'

Four

Actually, there were two of them coming out of the flying saucer. They could not have looked more alien. Their skin was vaguely scaly, brown; their heads were huge relative to their tiny bodies. Their faces were shaped in V's. Although their mouths and noses were tiny, their eyes were large, black, almond-shaped. Their legs and arms were bony, but they had big hands, and what looked like only four fingers, no thumb. They wore thin tan jumpsuits, a black belt that carried exotic tools. In their hands they appeared to carry weapons of some kind. As they stepped from their ship they both searched around, very alert.

'What's happening?' Cindy said from below.

'They're as disgusting as I imagined they would be,' Sally whispered.

'But they look friendly,' Watch said.

'Watch!' Sally hissed. 'They're carrying weapons.'

'Probably only for protection,' Watch said.

'Yeah, right,' Sally said. 'I bet they shoot first and ask questions later.'

Watch shook his head. 'They are obviously from a culture far more advanced than our own. I am sure they have left mindless violence far behind. I want to talk to them.'

'I don't know,' Adam said quietly. 'Their technology may be advanced, but that does not mean they will be friendly. For all we know, they could be here to collect specimens. Watch, you've talked about that before. We might be better to stay out of sight, and just see what happens. Oh, look, the other ship's light has gone off. I think I see another door forming.'

The second ship was also opening up. Another two aliens stepped from the saucer. They joined their buddies, who now stood by the water, beside their bicycles. The aliens gestured with their instruments at the bikes. They seemed to be carrying on a conversation but they were not talking, or making any other kind of sound. Watch had an explanation.

'They probably communicate using telepathy,' Watch said. 'Exchanging thoughts directly from mind to mind.'

'Do you think they can read our minds from here?' Sally asked, worried.

'Who knows?' Watch said. 'But I still want to make contact with them.'

'Why?' Adam asked. 'I think it's too risky.'

Watch shrugged. 'I want to go for a ride in one of their spaceships.' He moved to leave them. 'You guys can stay here.'

Sally grabbed his arm. 'Wait a second. They can see there are four bikes. They'll come looking for us, if they like the look of you, or even if they don't like your look. You're risking all of us with this mad idea.'

Watch spoke seriously. 'Why do we live in Spooksville? It's not just because our families live here. It's because this is a place of adventure. The unknown surrounds us every time we leave our homes. I know what I'm doing is dangerous. All great adventures are.'

Cindy was impressed. 'That was a nice speech, Watch.'

'If they capture you, and take you prisoner,' Adam said, 'I don't know if we'll be able to rescue you.' He gripped his friend's hand. 'If they take you inside their ship, we may never see you again.'

There was still a faint glow from the saucers. They could see Watch's face just enough to read his expression. For a moment he seemed touched, an unusual emotion for him.

Most of the time Watch showed as much emotion as, well, one of the aliens hanging out by the water.

'You would miss me?' he asked, surprised.

'We would miss you terribly, you major idiot,' Sally said.

'Be careful,' Cindy called out from below. 'Don't take any unnecessary risks.'

'The only way you can do that in this town is to stay in bed twenty-four hours a day,' Sally said. But she reached over and gave Watch a hug. 'Don't let them do any genetic experiments on you. You're fine the way you are, really.'

Adam shook Watch's hand. 'Shout for help if you think you're in trouble.'

'Just don't use our names,' Sally added.

Watch said goodbye and slowly walked down towards the reservoir. As soon as he was away from the rocks, the aliens looked over and raised what appeared to be their weapons. From the reaction of the aliens, it did not appear as if they knew Watch – and therefore the rest of them – had been there to begin with. Adam said as much to Sally and Cindy, who had now crawled up to the edge of the rocks so that she could see.

'That's probably true,' Sally said. 'But why is such an advanced race greeting Watch with pointed weapons?'

Adam was grim. 'Especially when he's holding out his

24

hands to show he's not armed. I don't like this.'

'He's such a brave boy,' Cindy whispered, anxious.

'He's a fool,' Sally remarked. 'A brave fool.'

The aliens may or may not have tried to communicate with Watch. From a distance of fifty metres it was hard to tell. It did appear as if Watch tried to talk to them, but Adam and his friends could not hear the telepathic thoughts the aliens may have responded with. However, the aliens certainly did not lower their weapons. Finally, after a couple of minutes of inspecting Watch from all angles, one of the aliens grabbed his arm and led him towards the door of the first saucer. Although Watch did not put up a fight, his friends got the impression he was being dragged into the ship. Sally and Adam and Cindy looked at each other anxiously.

'What are we going to do now?' Cindy asked.

'Well,' Sally said. 'He wanted to see the ship. Now he gets to see the ship.'

'He wants to go for a joy-ride in space,' Adam countered. 'He doesn't want to be dissected.' Adam shook his head. 'We can't just sit here and do nothing.'

'I have a bad feeling that we can do nothing against their ray-guns,' Sally said. 'Maybe we should call the President of the United States.'

'It will take us forever to reach a phone,' Adam said.

25

'We have to save Watch ourselves.' He went to get up. 'I'm going to speak to the aliens.'

Sally grabbed his arm and pulled him back down. 'You think you're going to have more success than Watch? Can't you see what's going on here? These aliens are here to collect genetic material to microscopically implant in their DNA to enrich and regenerate their ancient and failing species.'

'You can tell all that just by looking at them?' Cindy asked doubtfully.

Adam shook free of Sally. 'I don't want to walk out there any more than you want to. If you have a better plan, let's hear it.'

Sally thought for a moment. 'Nothing comes to me right away. But let's not act hastily. Let's wait and see what happens.'

What happened next as far as Watch was concerned was nothing. He did not reappear. But two of the aliens left the area around the reservoir and hiked back into the hills, not far from where Adam and his friends were crouched.

'They could be trying to encircle us,' Sally said.

Adam nodded darkly. 'We have to keep an eye on our backs. But if I am going to confront them, this might be the time, while they're at half strength.'

'I can't let you go out there alone,' Sally said.

'You can't come with me,' Adam said. 'Cindy's injured. Someone has to stay with her.'

'I'd rather you didn't go down there alone,' Cindy said. 'Take Sally with you.'

'I wasn't volunteering myself,' Sally complained. 'I was just speaking generally.' She paused and frowned. 'I suppose I could go with you, Adam. But I hate us not having a plan of action. We'll probably be taken prisoner like Watch and dragged to a distant planet circling a dying sun where we'll be dumped in a sterile prison and sliced open with a burning laser beam. Why, we're lambs going to slaughter.'

'You're not a lamb, Sally,' Cindy said.

'I was speaking poetically,' Sally said.

'Tell me what else to do,' Adam said.

'I don't know what else to do,' Sally snapped back. 'I just know that you can't trust gross-looking aliens with hand phasers.'

'They only have phasers on *Star Trek*,' Cindy said.

'How do we know these guys didn't write the TV show?' Sally asked.

Adam spoke wearily. 'We're getting nowhere with this arguing. I'm going down to demand that they release Watch. You can come if you want, Sally. But I don't think it's a good idea.'

'You mean it's all right for you to be a hero and not me?' Sally asked, getting to her feet. 'Really, Adam, you're a bit of a sexist. A girl can save the day just as easily as a boy.' She glanced at the saucers again. Only one alien stood visible, near the door of the first ship, the door through which Watch had disappeared. 'I wonder if there are boy aliens and girl aliens.'

'Right now I think that's the least of our worries,' Adam said.

'You never know,' Sally replied. She leaned over and patted Cindy on the back. 'If we don't come back, and you do manage to escape, write a book about me when you grow up. The world has to know what it lost tonight.'

Cindy was not in a joking mood. 'I wish you guys plenty of luck.'

Together, Adam and Sally crept from behind the rocks and walked slowly in the direction of the two saucers. The alien standing guard reacted quickly to their approach. Stepping towards them, he drew his weapon and pointed it at their heads. Adam and Sally put up their arms. Up close, the alien looked even more strange. It had no nails on its fingers, and not a trace of hair on its body. Its huge black eyes were completely devoid of emotion or feeling. They were so cold they could have belonged to an insect. Adam felt a sinking feeling in his chest. He doubted he would be able to reason with the creature.

'Hello,' Adam said. 'We come in peace. We mean you no harm. My name is Adam. This is my friend, Sally. Inside your flying saucer you have another friend of ours named Watch. We just want him back. That is all we want.'

'But we do have friends in high places,' Sally added. 'And they would avenge our deaths with great relish.'

'Shh,' Adam cautioned her. 'I don't know if it understands us.'

The alien just stared at them for a minute. Then it gestured with its weapon. It wanted them to walk into the flying saucer. Adam shook his head.

'No,' Adam said. 'We want our friend back. We don't want to go in your ship. Give him back to us and we won't bother you any more.'

'Yeah,' Sally added. 'And remember that you're a visitor to this planet. Show some manners, would ya?'

Apparently the alien didn't like Sally's tone. It took a step forward and grabbed her right arm. She shook it off – it did not appear that strong – but immediately it grabbed her again and pointed its weapon directly between her eyes. Sally recoiled in terror. That was enough for Adam. He was through talking. No more Mr Nice Human.

Adam launched himself at the alien.

The alien spun on him. Levelled its weapon.
Adam saw a flash of green light. Heard Sally scream.
Then everything went black.

Five

For Cindy, watching Adam and Sally fight with the alien
was the hardest thing she had ever done. Cindy knew
from the start the battle was hopeless. It especially hurt
that she could do nothing to help the others. A second
after the alien shot Adam, it turned its weapon on Sally.
To her credit, Sally did not turn and run. She tried to
attack the alien. But the creature was too quick for her.
The black instrument in its hand spurted another blast of
green light, and Sally collapsed on the ground beside
Adam.

Cindy didn't even know if either of them were still
alive.

She was not given long to grieve over her fallen pals.
Behind her she heard sounds further up the hill. The
other two aliens were either returning to their ship or else
closing in to take her captive. Sprained ankle or not, Cindy

swore to herself she would not be taken without a fight.

Climbing to her feet, hobbling on one foot, she listened closer, trying to determine the course of the aliens. They did not appear to be coming directly towards her. Instead they were following the path of a narrow valley that cut through the side of the hill where she was hiding. Actually, it was more of a ravine, cut by the winter rains. It was only thirty metres to her right. Cindy decided she would hide above the lip of the ravine and shower rocks down on the aliens as they came by. If she could get a hold of just one of their weapons, she thought, it would help even out the fight.

Trying her best to move silently, Cindy half hopped and half dragged herself to the edge of the ravine. She got there none too soon. The two aliens were almost directly below her. Grabbing hold of a watermelon-sized rock, she lifted it over her head. There was faint background light coming from the two saucers, although both ships were in dim mode. It helped her to aim, but here in the ravine it was poor shooting at best. As she let fly the first rock, she thought she would need a miracle to hit anything.

There was a flash of green light.

Cindy blinked. Had she been shot?

No. Quite the reverse.

Below her, the two aliens lay unconscious on the ground.

'But who shot them?' Cindy whispered aloud. Looking around, she couldn't find another soul, human or alien. Briefly she wondered if she had imagined the green light. Or maybe her rock had hit them, after all – both of them. Or perhaps one of their weapons had accidentally gone off when they struck the ground. It didn't really matter, she decided. She was taking their weapons now. She had fought with ghosts and hyeets. She could handle aliens.

Cindy hobbled down to where the aliens lay silent. They appeared stunned, not dead. She could hear them breathing. Quickly she stripped off their black belts, tucking one gun in her own belt while keeping the other ready in her right hand. She didn't know how these particular guns were set, if they would stun or kill when she fired them. But fire them she would, as soon as she got sight of that monster who'd shot Adam and Sally.

Cindy hobbled back to her position behind the rocks. But here there was no chance for her to rest. The alien and his partner were dragging Adam into the saucer. They could not be very strong. Even though there were two of them, they were struggling with Adam's lifeless body. But Cindy had no doubt they would come back for Sally in a minute. Unfortunately for Adam, they were already beside the saucer.

Cindy had a moment of panic. The ship was fifty metres away. She could not run there; she could hardly walk. On the other hand, she could not simply stand and start shooting, not without the risk of hitting Adam. But she had to do something and she had to do it now. People who went into that ship did not come out.

Cindy took aim. But not directly at the aliens. She aimed for the saucer itself. Pulling the trigger, she felt no recoil but saw a narrow flash of green light. It hit the side of the craft, and made the aliens jump. For a moment they dropped Adam and pointed in her direction. They raised their own weapons. For an instant, Cindy wondered if they took target practice in their home world – and whether their weapons were set to kill.

The large rock beside her exploded.

Cindy dived for cover. But after crawling a few feet to the side, she was back up again in a moment. So they wanted to play rough. Cindy twisted a tiny knob on her weapon all the way round in the other direction. Of course she did not know what the knob controlled, but she figured it might boost the weapon's power. Again she took aim at the saucer and pulled the trigger.

Her ray-gun was no longer set on stun.

The ship exploded with sparks as the green beam licked its surface. However, the hull of the saucer did not break. The ship was probably still capable of spaceflight. Cindy fired again, and got a similar violent response. But she was having to be very careful not to aim at the aliens or Adam, who were terribly exposed. At least she had a ton of rocks to hide behind. They took another couple of shots at her and set a bunch of dust flying, but they didn't even come close to hitting her. They appeared anxious to get inside and get away. Maybe they were not used to humans who fought back.

Grabbing Adam, they pulled him into the saucer.

Before Cindy could get off a third shot, the door vanished.

'No!' Cindy screamed, and jumped out from her place behind the rocks, almost falling over with her bad ankle. The saucer began to glow brightly. She knew it was preparing for take off. Raising her weapon once more, she took aim. This time she fired off a series of shots in quick succession. The saucer shook under the pounding, and smoke and sparks were everywhere. But Cindy should have realised that the saucer had weapons of its own. As it bobbled off the ground, it spun round and Cindy saw two green streaks rush along the perimeter of the ship towards each other. As they collided, a blinding beam of light flashed in her direction. Instinctively, Cindy dived to the side and half the hill behind her seemed to fly into the air in one gigantic explosion.

The noise was deafening, the shock wave crushing. If Cindy had not been flat on the ground, she surely would have been killed. As it was, she lay stunned for several moments, recovering only when the saucer was a vanishing white dot in the sky. She opened her eyes just as it blinked out of view.

'They got Adam,' she whispered. 'They got Watch.'

But they had not got Sally. Cindy found her lying unmoving, not far from the remaining saucer. Smoke and tiny fires littered the landscape. Sally had a pulse, she was breathing. Cindy hobbled to the water and soaked her own shirt in it. Then she returned to Sally and squeezed the water on to her friend's face. Sally opened her eyes with a start.

'That'd better not be water from the reservoir,' Sally said.

'It is,' Cindy said.

Sally sat up and wiped her face with the back of her arm. 'You'd better pray my face doesn't turn grey and my hair doesn't fall out,' she complained. 'Or else you're going to be bobbing for apples tomorrow night in a barrel of reservoir water.'

'They've taken Adam and Watch,' Cindy cried.

'Oh, my head hurts.' Sally rubbed her forehead. 'What are you talking about?'

'The aliens! Their ship left with them in it!'

Sally was instantly alert. She glanced around. 'Why didn't they take me?'

Cindy held up one of her weapons. 'I ambushed a couple of aliens and took their guns. They're lying over there in the ravine, unconscious.' Cindy paused and gestured to the remaining flying saucer. 'Why don't we drag them back to their own ship, wake them up and put a gun to their heads and demand that they go after Adam and Watch?'

Sally thought for a moment and smiled wickedly.

'Sounds like my kind of plan,' she said.

Six

When Adam came to, he was lying on his back. The first
thing he felt – besides the floor beneath him – was his
splitting headache. He could hear his pulse in his head. It
pounded like thunder. Every time his heart beat, it was as
if the nerves in his brain squeezed together. He felt so
awful he saw no point in even opening his eyes. But he
did anyway.

'How are you doing?' Watch asked, sitting beside him.
'Got a headache?'

Adam groaned. 'Yeah. How did you know?'

'I had the same thing when I woke up. I felt like my
skull was about to explode. I think I got zapped by the
same gun as you.'

Right then Adam remembered the alien and his nasty
weapon. He pulled himself into an upright position. It
took a moment before his vision settled down enough

that he could see straight. Immediately he thought he was imagining things.

He was inside an alien craft flying through space. The ship was not large. It was only about five metres from where he and Watch sat to the other side where the two aliens stood at an exotic control panel. Except for the controls, the interior was relatively featureless and rather dim. Adam had to squint to see clearly. The floor was a simple tan carpet. The walls were black and off-white in colour. The aliens had obviously not hired an interior decorator when they were building their ship. Every ninety degrees, on the side walls, was a small circular viewing screen.

But overhead was a glorious sight. The ceiling appeared to be one huge viewing portal. Adam had thought he had seen a lot of stars, sitting beside the reservoir. There had to be a hundred times that number now. The Milky Way seemed to shimmer with magical radiance. The unblinking stars looked close enough to touch. He wondered if they had already left the solar system. Watch shook his head.

'This ship changes orientation every few minutes,' he said. 'Not long ago I saw the sun through the ceiling. It's a lot smaller in size than seen from Earth but at least it's still there.'

'Do you know where we're headed?'

'Your guess is as good as mine. But I would assume we're returning to the aliens' home world.'

'Do you think it's in our solar system?' Adam asked.

'No. There isn't another planet in our solar system that can support life. It has to be around another star. It may not even be in our galaxy.'

'Great. What will we do there?' Adam said.

Watch shrugged. 'I try not to think about it.'

Adam nodded to the two aliens, who appeared to be ignoring them for the time being. 'Have they spoken to you?'

'No. They act as if I'm not even here. But I'm convinced they're telepathic. They communicate strictly in silence.'

'Do you think they can read our minds?' Adam asked.

'I'm not sure. If they can, I think they have to concentrate on us to pick up our thoughts. That's just an impression I get.'

Adam gestured to the absence of chains. 'How come they haven't tied us up?'

'We don't exactly have a lot of places we can run to.'

'You have a point there,' Adam agreed.

'Also, I think one blast of their guns was enough to let us know who's in charge. Is your head feeling any better?'

Adam rubbed his neck. 'Yeah, it's getting there.'

'The pain goes away pretty quickly, once you're awake.'

Adam remembered something. 'You know, just before I was shot, one of the aliens was wrestling with Sally. I wonder how she got away.'

'Maybe she didn't. Maybe she's aboard the other ship.'

'Have you seen it?' Adam asked.

'No. But I assume it isn't far behind us.'

Adam lowered his voice. 'Do you have an escape plan?'

'No.'

'You must have some ideas?'

Watch shook his head. 'Neither of us knows how to pilot this ship. We can't forcibly take over, even if they give us half a chance. We're stuck.'

'But I don't want to live the rest of my life on an alien planet.'

'The rest of your life might not be that long.'

'You're encouraging,' Adam complained.

'I'm sorry. I just can't imagine how we're going to get out of this. Unless the aliens decide to take us home. And I don't think that's likely. Not after they went to so much trouble to kidnap us.'

'Did they stun you as soon as you went in the ship?'

'No. Only when I tried to leave.' Watch nodded as if impressed. 'They've got pretty cool guns. I wonder what scientific principle they use.'

Just then a circular door appeared in the centre of the

floor, and a small alien, riding a narrow lift, appeared. He looked like a kid, although as far as Adam knew he might be ten thousand years old. Like the others, he had a huge head, even though his big black eyes did not seem as cold. He stared at them for a moment and then walked over. He seemed to bow slightly as he stopped near their feet. He couldn't have been half a metre tall.

'Hello,' Adam said flatly. 'What's your name? Or do you just have a number?'

To Adam's immense surprise, a reply immediately formed in his mind. It was not a thought of his own. The texture and clarity of it was much sharper. It was almost as if a miniature being had crawled inside his brain and shouted something aloud. The unspoken words definitely came from the creature in front of them.

'My name is a combination of syllables and numbers. I am Ekwee12. Who are you?'

Adam had to take a deep breath. The reply had startled him, yet also pleased him. He had not been looking forward to spending the rest of his days with mute aliens.

'I'm Adam, and this is my friend Watch.'

The alien continued to stare at him with his big eyes. His face showed no emotion. *'What is your number?'*

'We don't have numbers where we come from,' Adam said.

'What is your rating then?'

'We don't have ratings either,' Adam added. 'But I will be in seventh grade next year. Hopefully.'

'I don't think they have junior high where we're heading,' Watch muttered.

The alien glanced at Watch. 'What is junior high?'

'It's a type of school,' Adam said. 'It means you're too old to play with toys, but not old enough to drive a car.'

'What is a car? A vehicle of transportation?'

'Yes,' Adam said. 'We have them on our planet.' He nodded to the other two aliens, who continued to ignore them. 'How are you related to those two guys?'

'They are teachers. This is an educational trip for me.'

Adam spoke bitterly. 'Are they teaching you to kidnap innocent people?'

The alien hesitated. For a moment the skin around his mouth seemed to wrinkle. He glanced at the aliens behind him and then back at them.

'Explain the word kidnap?'

'It means we have been taken against our will,' Adam said. 'Your teachers knocked us out with their weapons. I was dragged unconscious aboard this ship. Didn't you see any of this happen?'

Again the alien paused. He seemed to be thinking.

'No. I was told to stay below after we landed.'

'But you believe our story, don't you?' Adam asked, for he sensed that the little alien did not approve of what had been done. Once more the alien took a moment before answering.

'You do not appear to be lying.'

'We're telling you what happened,' Watch said. 'We were attacked by your people.'

'You are not hurt.'

'But we are held captive,' Watch said. 'We want to go home.'

'We are going home.'

'We want to go to *our* home,' Adam said. 'Back to where we were picked up.' He paused. 'Can you help us?'

The little alien lowered his head. *'I am just a student. I am not in charge here.'*

'But maybe you could talk to your teachers,' Adam said. 'Explain to them that we are upset.'

The little alien glanced over his shoulder. *'They would not listen.'*

Adam was curious. 'Are they listening to us now?'

The little alien closed his eyes briefly. It was the first time they had seen his eyelids. They were faintly translucent, pretty weird-looking. When he opened his eyes again, Adam thought he saw a faint spark in those black depths.

45

'No. They are not listening. They do not care about you two. Also, among my people, the young are better telepaths. My telepathic range is twice theirs.'

'That's interesting,' Adam said. 'I thought it would have been the other way around. Why are kids better at picking up and sending thought?'

'We have less stress.'

'We seem to be picking up speed,' Watch said. 'But even going this fast, I don't see how we're going to reach your home planet in the next century. Can you explain how this craft works?'

'This ship first accelerates to near light speed. Then we convert our momentum to pure energy and use the power to jump through hyperspace. We can only make such a jump far from the gravitational pull of the Sun.'

'Can we cross many light years in a single hyperjump?' Watch asked.

The alien hesitated as if for once he did not understand the question. 'Yes. We can travel any distance, if it is necessary.'

'What does all this mean?' Adam asked Watch.

'That we're in serious trouble,' Watch replied. 'If we don't reverse our course before the hyperjump, I doubt we'll ever get home.'

'When do we jump through hyperspace?' Adam asked the little alien.

The alien consulted a small instrument fastened to his wrist. *'Fifteen of your minutes.'*

Adam was aghast. 'That's so soon.' He tried to keep his voice steady, yet he spoke with passion. 'Do you care about us? Can you help us escape?'

The little alien may have tried to smile then. Once more the tan flesh around his tiny narrow mouth creased. He probably shouldn't have bothered. His expression looked anything but friendly. But Adam sensed his good intentions.

'I care that your free will may have been violated. That is against the laws of our people. I do not understand how our teachers could have committed such a violation.'

'You should point that out to them,' Watch suggested.

But the alien repeated his earlier comment. *'They would not listen.'*

Adam was sympathetic. 'Adults don't listen to kids in your world either? It's the same where we come from. We have plenty of smart things to say but we're not even allowed to vote for who is president of our country.' Adam paused. He spoke in a whisper. 'Do you know how to fly this ship?'

'Yes.'

'Can you help us escape?' Adam asked again, not wanting to push the guy but worried about the coming

47

hyperjump. 'We really have to get home. My mother's already made me dinner by now. She'll be wondering where I am.'

The little alien seemed to understand.

'I have a mother as well. She is nice to me.' The alien glanced once more at the others. He seemed lost in thought, or perhaps even in confusion. He sent them a final mental communication. *'I will have to consider the situation.'*

The alien turned and stepped to where the others stood. They acknowledged his arrival with a slight nod of their two fat heads, but if they communicated with the little guy Adam and Watch did not hear it, with their ears or their minds. Adam continued to fret about the hyperjump.

'What do you know about hyperspace?' he asked Watch.

Watch shrugged. 'Our scientists only have theories that it even exists. But it sounds like this ship is capable of sliding into a short cut through space. That's what hyperspace must be. This ship uses the energy of its tremendous speed to open the door to the short cut.'

'Then we have to brake somehow,' Adam said.

'You can throw one of your shoes at the control panel, but I don't think that will do the trick,' Watch said. 'It will probably just get you shot again. And this time they might not have their guns on stun.'

Adam went to stand. 'I'm tired of just sitting here doing

nothing. I'd rather go down fighting.'

Watch grabbed his arm. 'We have to be patient. The little guy clearly wants to help us. Let's give him a chance.'

Reluctantly Adam sat down again. 'I'll give him ten minutes, that's all.'

But he didn't have to wait that long. Five minutes later, the other flying saucer suddenly appeared. They saw it through the transparent ceiling. It swooped dangerously close, glowing brightly, and as it did an angry burst of green light struck the ceiling. For a moment, Adam and Watch were blinded. Their own flying saucer shook violently as the lights dimmed further. Adam thought he smelt smoke.

The two aliens at the controls gestured excitably, although they didn't say a word. They probably could speak if they wanted to. They had radio communication – Adam and Watch knew that for a fact a minute later, when they heard Sally's voice come through the hidden speakers.

'This is Captain Sara Wilcox and Lieutenant Cindy Makey of the Starship UFO. We demand your complete and unconditional surrender. You have two Earth minutes to comply. Failure to do so will result in your immediate and total destruction.'

Adam and Watch looked at each other in amazement.

Seven

Aboard Starship UFO – the name as well as their respective ranks had been Sally's idea – Cindy wondered if Sally had pushed it too far. Behind them, against the far wall, the two aliens huddled together as if afraid. Cindy worried they knew something their human enemies did not.

'Maybe we should negotiate a trade of prisoners,' Cindy said.

'This is interstellar war,' Sally said, her finger on the firing button. 'I don't negotiate.'

'But if you blow up their ship, you'll kill Adam and Watch,' Cindy pointed out.

Sally removed her finger from the firing button. They had figured out how to work the weapons – and navigate the vessel – on the journey out from the Sun. Of course the aliens had given them a few practical hints – when Sally had held the guns to their heads. Sally was showing the aliens no mercy. She yelled at them constantly, threatening to boot them out into deep space, where they would surely die. Cindy did not approve of the cruelty, even though the aliens would probably have killed them if given the chance.

'I know that,' Sally said. 'But I have to bluff with conviction. If I don't, Adam and Watch will never escape.'

'You don't know that for sure. A gentle approach might be better.'

Sally shook her head. 'Look who we're dealing with. These aliens land on our planet and immediately whip out their guns and kidnap our friends. We have to meet force with force. It's the only way.'

'Does it occur to you that the aliens in the other ship have a thousand times more experience at interstellar combat than you? What if they blow us out of the sky?'

Sally nodded. 'I thought of that. That's why I hit them hard first. I'm hoping we've already disabled their weapon systems.'

Cindy pointed to the large viewing screen above. 'You'd better pray as well as hope. They're coming around. And from the green glow around their sides, it looks like they're firing up their weapons.'

Sally spun on their captive aliens with a gun in hand. 'How do we raise our shields?' she demanded.

The aliens looked at each other with their big eyes. They shook their heads minutely, trembling as they did so, and hugged each other closer. They had earlier communicated with Sally and Cindy telepathically, but now they seemed too scared to send a clear thought.

'I think they're saying we don't have any shields,' Cindy said.

'We have to have shields!' Sally shouted. 'This is a spaceship. They always have shields in the movies.'

A hard blast, thick as a fist, struck their ship. Sally and Cindy went flying, and hit the floor. For a moment their lights failed and they were plunged into total darkness. It was terrifying; they could have been floating in empty space. Fortunately an emergency system came on, flooding the interior with a sober red light. Sally and Cindy crawled to their knees. Cindy felt a twinge in her right ankle. In all the excitement she had almost forgotten she was injured.

'They'll pay for that,' Sally said bitterly. She reached for the control panel, the firing button. 'We're taking no prisoners.'

Cindy stopped her. 'Wait a second. I hear something.'

'What?' Sally demanded.

'A telepathic message. Listen, here it comes again.'

'Push the green button. Then the purple one.'

'Did you hear that?' Cindy asked.

'Yeah, So what?' Sally pointed to the two quivering aliens, whose big black eyes looked ready to burst from their heads. 'They're just giving us instructions to blow ourselves up.'

Cindy got to her feet. 'They're more afraid of dying than us. The thought's not coming from them. It must be coming from the other ship.'

Sally was disgusted. 'Like we're going to listen to an order from them? Are you out of your mind? I say we return fire. If we lose Adam and Watch then at least they died in a good cause.' Once again she reached for the firing button. 'I'm locking on all our weapons. I'm going to maintain fire until one of us explodes.'

Cindy stopped her again. 'That's insane. We're *not* killing Adam and Watch.' She suddenly paused and went still. 'This thought feels different from the others. The person sending it seems to want to help us.'

Sally threw her arms in the air. 'The person sending this message is an alien! We can't trust it!'

Cindy spoke firmly. 'And we can't just keep blasting away. I say we give this message a chance. I know that sounds insane but somehow I trust it.'

Sally turned away in disgust. She glanced up at the ceiling. The other ship was coming round again. Sally could see them energizing their weapons.

'If you're going to respond to it, then you had better do so now,' Sally grumbled.

Cindy stepped to the control panel and pushed a green button, followed by a purple one. There was only one button of each colour on the panel. At first nothing happened. The other ship continued to bear down on them, its powerful weapon batteries glowing with a deadly green light. Then, behind her, Sally let out a gasp. Cindy whirled to see a little alien stand in the centre of their ship.

'Where did you come from?' Cindy exclaimed.

'You just teleported me from the other ship. I am here to help you and your friends, Adam and Watch. May I use the control panel please?'

'No!' Sally shouted, pointing her gun at the little alien. 'We're not turning over our ship to a runt like you.'

The alien stared at her calmly. 'I understand your lack of trust. I apologise for what my teachers have done so far to you and your friends. It is against our highest laws to infringe the free will of other intelligent creatures. I am here to help set the situation right. To do so, you must let me send a signal to the other ship. They will think I have taken control of this vessel and they won't fire upon it again. But if you don't let me take control, this ship, and you, will be destroyed in the next ten of your seconds.'

'Let him do it!' Cindy cried.

'No!' Sally argued. 'It could be a trap!'

'We're already trapped!' Cindy shouted back. She glanced overhead. The other ship was still the same distance away. 'We have no choice, Sally. Can't you see that? Lower your gun.'

Sally hesitated, then angrily turned away. 'This is your call, Cindy. If you're wrong, I'm never going to let you live it down.'

'If I'm wrong, you and I won't be alive to live anything down.' Cindy nodded to the little alien, who was waiting patiently in the centre of the floor for their decision. 'Do what you have to do. Hurry!'

The alien stepped up to the control panel. He pressed a series of buttons. Outside, above them, the other ship suddenly veered off. Cindy let out a cry of relief, but Sally was far from happy. She pointed a finger at the little alien.

'I want our friends released right now,' she said. 'Then I want us taken back to Earth.'

The little alien stared at them as he spoke in their minds. *That is not possible right now. I have no control over what my teachers on the other ship wish to do. And in a few of your minutes, they plan to jump through hyperspace and return to our home world. It is my suggestion that you allow me to follow them.*

'What?' Sally cried, raising her weapon once more. 'Do you think that we're so primitive we'd fall for such a scam? If we go through hyperspace – whatever that is – we'll never get home. You turn this ship around right now. We're going back to Earth.'

'Sally, you have to control your temper,' Cindy said. 'It clouds your reasoning. We can't go home yet. We have to go where Adam and Watch go. And I trust this little guy.' She spoke directly to the alien. 'When we reach your home world, do you think we can get our friends released?'

The alien hesitated. *'It is possible. I have a plan. But it is a dangerous plan.'*

Sally shook her head. She continued to point her gun at the alien. 'Why should we trust you?' she demanded. 'Why should you betray your own kind to help us?'

'I do not betray my own kind by doing what is right. If my teachers are breaking our laws, then I am helping them by calling the criminal act to their attention. Also, I have studied your kind since I was very young. I have always admired you. I wish only to be of service.'

'A likely story,' Sally muttered. She glanced at Cindy. 'How can you trust a runt with such a fat head?'

Cindy reached over and patted the little alien on the head. The guy seemed to enjoy the attention. He moved a step closer to her, and touched her leg with his funny four-fingered hand.

'I don't know, I think he's kind of cute,' Cindy said. 'In a strange way, he reminds me of Adam.'

Sally snorted. 'If we get out of this, I'm going to tell Adam you said that.'

The alien looked at both of them. *I should think Adam would be happy to be compared to me.*

The situation was desperate. They were lost in space with aliens from another planet, and their friends were being held captive. But both Sally and Cindy suddenly burst out laughing. They could just imagine what Adam would say to that.

Eight

For Adam and Watch the jump through hyperspace proved unremarkable. They were racing into deep space – with the Sun now a bright star far behind them – when the aliens pushed a few buttons and there was a low hum. It lasted for only an instant. Adam felt as if everything went momentarily black. He felt a slight jerk; he might have twitched. Then he blinked and everything was exactly as it was before, only now the bright star was in front of them instead of behind.

'I thought the scenery would have changed more,' Adam muttered.

'So did I,' Watch said, puzzled.

'Are we sure we made the jump through hyperspace?'

'It seemed like it. Something happened.' Watch studied the stars through the wide ceiling. 'Maybe their solar system is not so far from our solar system, after all. Many of the constellations still look the same.'

'Are they the same?' Adam persisted.

'No. There are definite changes. For example, the Plough is bent out of shape. We must be seeing it from another angle. We have definitely travelled several light years in the last few seconds. But . . .' Watch trailed off.

'But what?'

Watch shook his head. 'I don't know what it is. Something is wrong here. I wish we still had our little friend to ask questions. I wonder where he went.'

'I get the impression he was teleported to the other ship. Notice how he stood real still in the exact centre of the floor. It was like he sent a mental signal to the girls to pick him up. Remember how he said his telepathic abilities had greater range than the adult aliens?'

'Do you think he's working for us?' Watch said.

'I hope so. Hey, that was pretty cool the way Sally just opened fire.'

'Yeah, she has guts. But she almost got us killed. I hope they follow us through hyperspace.'

'So do I,' Adam agreed. 'I think the little alien is our only ally in this part of the universe.'

Time crept slowly by. Adam and Watch began to feel hungry and thirsty. They complained to their captors but were completely ignored. Adam talked again about trying to jump the aliens, but he was now too tired to make the effort. Also, the more time that went by, the more he began to believe that the little alien was definitely in the other ship, and following them. Unfortunately they could see no sign of the other vessel. Perhaps that wasn't important. It was a big universe. The ship would have to be extremely close to be visible.

The sun up ahead continued to grow in brilliance. When it was about the same size as the Sun, seen from Earth, they saw a blue-white planet, with a silver moon circling round it. At first glance Adam thought he was seeing the Earth, but a closer look showed him that the continents and oceans were nothing like those of home. He felt a stab of despair. Even when everything had looked hopeless in the Haunted Cave, he had still been able to make constructive decisions. Here he was completely help-less. He had only a kid alien to rely on. Beside him, Watch pointed at the planet.

'See those glittering silver shapes orbiting it?' Watch said. 'I think each of them is either a space station or a space ship. This culture must be extremely advanced. Some of them look huge.'

'Maybe the aliens live in space,' Adam suggested. 'Maybe they polluted their planet so badly they can't live on the ground.'

'The way the human race is going, that might happen to us,' Watch said.

'If this alien race doesn't destroy us first,' Adam said. 'I've been thinking of the bigger picture. Our lives may not be all that is at stake here. What if they're preparing a huge invasion of our planet? What if they kidnapped us so they can torture us for what we know?'

'But we don't know anything,' Watch said.

'That's true – but they may not understand that. For all they know, kids from Spooksville may be the ruling class on planet Earth.'

'We certainly see more weird things than anybody else back home.' Watch continued to stare at the approaching planet and the silver chain of floating space ships and space stations. 'Your pollution theory might not be far-fetched. See that brown murky junk near that coast?'

'Yeah.'

'That looks like smog to me. Really bad smog. It's amazing, for all their advanced technology, that they haven't been able to clean it up.'

'It's easier to prevent a spill than to clean one up,' Adam said philosophically. 'But personally I don't care how messed up their world is. I just want to get home and have dinner.'

'Turkey and mashed potatoes would be nice right now,' Watch agreed.

'Is that what your aunt was cooking tonight?' Adam knew Watch did not live with either of his parents, or even with his little sister. But he had never asked his friend why the family was not together. The subject seemed too touchy. Watch lowered his head. 'My aunt never cooks,' he said softly. 'I have to prepare all my own food.'

Adam reached over and patted him on the back. 'You can come to my house any time for dinner. You're always welcome.'

Watch looked up and smiled faintly. 'You're only telling me that now your house is billions of miles away.'

Adam had to chuckle. 'Listen, when we were playing cards, how did you know Sally was bluffing? She acted exactly as if she had a strong hand.'

'The cards are marked.'

Adam was shocked. 'What? You mean you cheated?'

'Yes.'

'But that's terrible. Why play if you're going to cheat?'

'I can't see people's expressions as well as you guys can. So I mark the cards just to make it even.'

'Oh,' Adam said. 'When you explain it that way, I guess it isn't really cheating.'

'You can have your rocks back if you want.'

'That's all right. I'm not that into rocks.'

Watch pointed at one of the small viewing screens on the walls. 'See that huge cylindrical station? I think that's our destination. Look at the size of it! The station must be a mile long.'

Watch was right. The alien station was breathtaking in its size and obvious sophistication. It was like unto a miniature world in itself. And the most amazing thing was that there were thousands of others just like it in orbit.

The station rotated on its axis. But the flying saucer, as it approached, did not strive to match the station's speed, not exactly. It seemed as if they were going to enter the station from the top, in the centre, where there was no obvious movement at all. Suddenly a wide black door materialised in front of them. Adam was reminded of a hungry mouth, ready to swallow them. The saucer moved towards it. He shook his head sadly.

'Even if the little alien is helping us,' he said, 'I don't see how he can get us out of here.'

'It does look hopeless,' Watch agreed. 'But it usually does when you live in Spooksville.'

'We're a long way from Spooksville,' Adam grumbled.

The saucer flew into the station. For a moment all was dark. Then they came out into a massive chamber lit with soft yellow light. The wide space was a parking lot for saucers just like theirs. Literally hundreds floated nearby. Smoothly, their pilot manoeuvred past them. They seemed to be heading towards a dock of some kind. Adam knew that in a minute they would be leaving the ship. This deepened his depression. At least inside the spaceship, they had always had the chance of turning round and going home. Now that did not look on the cards.

There came a soft bump. The ship went completely still.

A door materialised to their left.

It led into a seemingly endless hallway.

The two aliens turned and drew their weapons.

The message was clear. Get up and get going.

Adam and Watch slowly stood and looked at each other.

'Are we having fun yet?' Adam asked.

'Sure,' Watch said. 'So much fun we might die laughing.'

The aliens escorted them from the flying saucer.

Nine

Sally and Cindy had indeed followed Adam and Watch through hyperspace. With the little alien's help, they were keeping far enough away to remain invisible. Yet Cindy believed the aliens on Adam's ship thought *her* ship's control had been returned to the aliens – the two cowards Sally had finally locked in the basement. Their pal had given that impression. He was trying to act like the hero in the fight between the aliens and the humans. Yet, although Cindy trusted him, she worried that Sally might be right. Maybe he was simply leading them into a trap.

But he seemed so sincere. As they ploughed towards his home world, he asked so many questions. They discovered he had been studying them since he was old enough to read.

'Why were you up in the hills by the water?'

'We were trying to cool off,' Cindy said. 'It's been hot

in our home town lately. We rode our bikes up to the reservoir. Did you see them?'

'No. Just before landing, my teachers made me go below.'

'They just didn't want you to see how cruel they are,' Sally muttered.

'That may be true, and if it is, I am disturbed. A report to our government must be made. The people must know what is happening.'

Sally snorted. 'On our world, if you make a report to the government, that's the last you hear about it. It's much better to get on TV.'

'I know your TV. I have studied it. You watch different shows. Some of them involve space travel, although your race is not yet advanced to travel much further than Earth orbit.'

'We've been to the Moon,' Cindy said. 'We might go to Mars soon.'

'If you know about our TV,' Sally said, 'you must have seen our programmes about you guys. We know about you aliens. We know you float down in the middle of the night and mutilate our cattle and steal our children. You can't underestimate us. If you try to invade, we won't be taken by surprise.'

The little alien paused and stared at her. 'I am not an alien. Do you not know that?'

Cindy spoke quickly. 'What Sally means is that you

appear alien to us. I'm sure on your home world you look just fine. There, *we* would be the aliens.'

'*You would not be alien to us. That is not possible.*'

'Then your people must be more accepting than ours,' Cindy said.

'They sure aren't any less violent,' Sally grumbled.

The alien lowered his head. '*My people are not perfect. We have our problems.*'

Time went by. Up ahead, the alien sun continued to grow in size as they flew towards the heart of the solar system. About three hours after they'd made the hyperjump, they caught sight of a blue-white world. Cindy and Sally were surprised to see that it had a moon circling it just like their own moon. For a moment the girls wondered if they hadn't simply flown in a huge circle. But it was not the case; they were far from home. Studying the planet, they didn't recognize a single one of the continents.

The little alien steered them towards a huge space station.

'Are you sure this is where Adam and Watch were taken?' Cindy asked as they neared the massive structure.

'*Yes.*'

'How do you know?' Sally demanded.

'*I was informed by what you call radio.*'

'Can the two aliens we have stowed in the basement communicate telepathically with your government and warn them that we have taken over this space ship?' Sally asked.

'I have erected a mental shield around this ship. I have set it so that only my thoughts are allowed in and out.'

'What do your people intend to do with Adam and Watch?' Cindy asked.

The huge space station was very near. They were coming in at the top. A black doorway opened before them.

'I do not know.'

'What reason did your teachers give you for going to our home?' Sally asked.

'They said we went there to observe. To learn.'

The ship slowed to a crawl. They began to enter the station.

'Well, I hoped they learned not to mess with us,' Sally replied. 'You said you had a plan to rescue our friends. What is it?'

'It is hard to explain.'

Sally fingered the weapon she kept tucked in her belt. 'You're going to have to do better than that. I have trusted you this far, but before I leave this ship I want to know what you have up your sleeve.'

The alien appeared puzzled. He checked his sleeve.

'I have nothing up it except my arm, Sally.'

Sally snorted. 'Just tell me how we're going to get our friends out of this metal cylinder.'

The alien thought for a moment.

'None of us is going to leave this ship. Not right now. I am going to try and start what you call a riot.'

'What?' Cindy gasped.

'I am going to broadcast the thought that your friends have been taken by force and are being held captive. I have explained that this act violates our most important laws. But I can only do this once I know where your friends are, and once I am hooked into what you would call a youth computer network. Except this network works with telepathy, not electric modems such as you have in your present day culture.'

Sally glanced at Cindy. 'Did you get all that?' Sally asked.

'I don't know.' Cindy spoke to the alien. 'Why do you first have to know where Adam and Watch are?'

'Young people play pranks in our culture as they do in your culture. I will have to prove that your friends are being held captive. The best way to do this is to direct as many individuals my age as possible to the place where Adam and Watch are.'

'What if they are in a restricted area?' Sally asked.

'Nowhere in our culture is supposed to be restricted.'

'Why do you have to be hooked up to a network?' Sally

demanded. 'Why can't you just broadcast the information with your fat head . . . I mean, just with your incredible telepathic abilities?'

'It is easier on the network. It is set up so that interference is filtered out. I will be able to reach many more people this way.'

'When you say a riot, do you mean that hordes of your kind will begin to loot and burn?' Sally asked.

The idea seemed to startle the alien. He took a moment to respond.

'No. I mean that my people will gather and demand that Adam and Watch are released. It is the only way I can think of.'

Sally glanced at Cindy and shook her head. 'I think our little friend underestimates what his government has going on the side.'

'What do you mean?' Cindy asked.

'Think about it. These ships obviously landed in Spooksville with the purpose of taking hostages. The aliens we hijacked weren't there to explore. They were there to grab some humans, pure and simple. That means they must have done it before, many times.'

'What are you saying?' Cindy asked.

'I am finally beginning to believe this runt is on our side. But I think he is naive. His government is no better than any government on Earth. It's up to all kinds of secret stuff that he knows nothing about. That's why they hid him out of the way when we were being kidnapped. Ten to one he's never going to be able to find out where Adam and Watch have been taken, especially if he stays inside this ship.' Sally paused. 'Did you hear that . . . What is your name anyway?'

'Ekwee12.'

'Do you mind if I call you Ek?' Sally said. 'No? Good. Did you hear what I just said?'

'Yes.'

'Well, what do you think?'

'I hope you are wrong.'

Sally had to laugh, but it was not a happy laugh. 'You can hope all you want. But I think we'll all be lucky to get out of this alive. One thing is for sure. As soon as we dock, there will be a group of guards waiting for us outside.'

'No. I have already sent a message ahead that I have taken control of this ship. That is what I told my teachers on the other ship that I was going to do. There will be no guards waiting for us.'

'Ek, I hate to tell you this,' Sally said. 'But you're about to get your first lesson in the real universe. This ship fired on the other ship. That is no small matter. Guards will be waiting for us and they will be armed. As soon as we dock, I want you to let them in and Cindy and I are going to hide behind the side of the wall. As soon as they're visible, we're going to stun them and then lock them in the basement with the other goons. In fact, would you set our guns to the right setting? I don't want to accidentally kill the guards. I would feel bad about it afterwards.'

Ek had to put a hand to his head. *'You will just shoot them if they come in?'*

'Yes,' Sally said. 'Listen, one of your guys already shot me tonight. And I woke up with a splitting headache. I have a right to a little retaliation.'

Ek gestured in front of them. *'We are about to dock. I should be able to tap into the network from here. I hope you are wrong about all this, Sally.'*

Ten

Adam and Watch were led to a sort of locker-room where they were told – telepathically – to undress and shower under a strange orange liquid. Actually, after all the bike riding and alien fighting, the shower was rather pleasant. The liquid was warm and smelt nice. Adam was happy to wash the dirt out of his hair.

But while they were in the shower, their clothes were taken. In their place was laid out two tan jump suits, similar to what the aliens wore, only larger. That was fine; neither of them was particularly attached to their clothes. They dressed quickly, enjoying the feel of the soft material against their skin. The only trouble was that Watch's glasses were missing. He stumbled about the room while Adam looked for them. The two observing aliens just stood there like statues, holding their ray-guns. Finally Adam got fed up.

'All right,' he said. 'What did you do with my friend's glasses? He needs them. He can't even walk down your long halls without them.'

At first the aliens acted like they didn't understand. They gestured with their guns for Adam and Watch to go through a door on the far side of the room. But Adam refused.

'We are not going anywhere until he gets his glasses back.' Adam pointed to his own eyes, then pointed at Watch's eyes. 'Understand? He uses those things to see.'

The aliens gestured again with their guns.

'No.' Adam crossed his arms over his chest. 'You're going to have to shoot us both. We are not leaving without those glasses.'

'Maybe you should tell them that they can shoot you if they want,' Watch said, bumping into a wall.

But the ultimatum worked. Finally they received a telepathic message.

'We did not know the glasses were so important.'

The glasses were returned and they were led from the locker-room area to a small cubicle that was equipped with an Earth-like toilet and two small beds set near the floor. The far wall of the room was made from what looked like clear glass or plastic; they could see through it into what appeared to be a courtyard. The moment they were inside

76

the tiny room, the aliens turned and left, locking the door behind them. Adam pounded on it for several seconds, then gave up in frustration. There was not even a door knob he could try to break.

'This is a cage,' Adam muttered.

'It's one of many cages,' Watch said, standing near the far wall. 'Look out there.'

The courtyard was really a circular collection of twenty similar rooms. Each was equipped with a similar transparent wall, and held a different creature from a strange world. Some cells held two of the same species. In one glance, Adam and Watch were treated to an overview of many life forms from the local galaxy.

Closest to them was a creature that seemed to have six heads. Two metres tall, it was vaguely insectile; it walked about on six legs and had dozens of eyes on three of its heads, and tiny claws and mouths on the remaining three. It stared at them wickedly, with its many claws snapping repeatedly. Instinctively, Adam and Watch backed away from their transparent wall. The thing looked like it wanted to eat them.

In another cage was a blob-like being that seemed to flow from one corner of its container to another. There were fish creatures, birdmen, and one individual that looked like a cross between a robot and a dinosaur. They even saw what they thought was a hyeet – a Bigfoot. The hairy ape-like fellow waved to them. Adam waved back without enthusiasm.

'We're in a zoo,' he said miserably.

'I wonder,' Watch said, 'where all the tourists are?'

'Maybe it's night-time.'

'You wouldn't have night-time aboard a space station. People probably work in shifts. If this is a zoo, I would think it would be open all the time.'

'What are you saying?' Adam asked.

Watch scratched his head. The aliens had taken his four watches, and not returned them with his glasses. Adam knew how much his friend missed them. They were like part of his body, his persona even. Of course, if there was no night and day on a space station, then there were really no time zones either. Watch had an accepting nature. He had not complained of the theft.

'I think this is more of a laboratory,' Watch said finally. 'I think we're cut off from the public.'

Adam frowned. 'That sounds terrible. Do you think they will experiment on us?'

Watch nodded. 'It's a possibility. We have to mentally prepare ourselves to have our organs removed, maybe without anaesthesia.'

'If they remove many of our organs, we'll die.'

'It might be a blessing.'

Adam stepped back from the transparent wall and sat down on one of the beds. He was completely exhausted. The time he had spent unconscious from the ray-gun zap did not qualify as a refreshing nap. He was also deathly thirsty and hungry. He wondered what the meals would be like.

'You're depressing me,' Adam muttered.

'I'm sorry.' Watch sat on the bed across from him. 'Maybe it's not as hopeless as it appears. We've been in some nasty fixes before. We've always escaped. Why should this time be any different?'

'Because this time we're trapped in a cage billions of miles from Earth?'

Watch yawned and leaned back on the bed. 'Now you're depressing me.'

There was nothing else to say, for the time being.

They both laid down and rested. They may have even dozed.

Time went by. They were not sure how much.

Then they heard a soft knock at the door.

'Hey. Are you in there?'

Eleven

As Sally had predicted, when they docked there were four guards waiting for them. Sally got Ekwee12 to invite them in and Cindy and Sally stunned them from behind. They stored the guards in the basement with the other two aliens. To everyone's immense relief, no other guards rushed to the scene. Perhaps Ekwee12 was partially right. Their people were no experts when it came to security. There was time to work.

Unfortunately, Ekwee12 was making little progress with his plan. They had been in space dock an hour and he was still unable to locate Adam and Watch. He was searching through some kind of computer map, projected on to a three-dimensional computer screen located to the left side of the control panel. He said it was supposed to register all living creatures on the station, including ones like them.

'I do not understand why they do not show up.'

'It's like I told you,' Sally said, as she paced behind the Ekwee12. 'There are restricted areas aboard this station. You have to forget about trying to find them. Just broadcast on your telepathic network what has happened. Maybe one of the thousands of fat-heads . . . I mean, maybe one of your many network partners will have an idea where they can be found.'

'I don't know if that's a good idea,' Cindy said. 'The moment Ek makes such a broadcast, more guards will show up here.'

Sally was animated. 'I know that. I'm not stupid. But they're going to come here anyway. At least we will have got the message out. Once they arrest us, there will be no chance. We'll probably be put to immediate death.'

Our culture does not have the death penalty.

'You don't know what your culture does behind closed doors,' Sally snapped. Then she paused, thinking. 'How can we protect ourselves inside this ship? When they do come for us?'

We can lock the door. But they will burn through it quickly, if they want to.

'Can you fire this ship's weapons while we're in space dock?' Sally asked.

That would not be a good idea. Many could be hurt.

Sally rolled her eyes. 'Like I'm worried about a few

casualties. Listen, Ek, I am not a violent person by nature, but you guys started this, and I intend to finish it. When your authorities show up, we need something to fight them with until we can get Adam and Watch back. Better yet, we need something to *force* them to give us our friends back. Even if we just use it as a bluff.'

'What is a bluff?'

'It's what you do when you want to win at poker,' Sally said. She pointed to the floor beneath them. 'This ship accelerated to near light speed in two hours. It must have a powerful engine or warp drive on board. What's its source of energy?'

'Our space drive is powered by the decay of an element called Zelithium 110. It cannot be found on your periodic table of elements because it does not exist naturally, except in the corona of extremely hot blue stars. As the element decays in a chamber of Hyperzoid Quartz, it radiates sub-atomic particles we call Bostonians. They are very powerful but unstable, unless carefully controlled.'

Sally glanced at Cindy. 'I got less than half of that,' Cindy said.

'You say the Bostonians are unstable?' Sally said. 'I like things that way. They bring out my finer moments. Tell me, Ek, can this stuff be used to make a bomb?'

Ekwee12 looked as worried as an expressionless alien

could. *Yes. The Hyperzoid Quartz can be tampered with so that the decay of Bostonians builds towards a critical mass.'*

'What happens when a critical mass is reached?' Sally asked.

'There is a huge explosion.'

'Would the explosion be strong enough to destroy this space station?' Sally asked.

Ekwee12 hesitated. *'Yes. And many stations and vessels in the immediate vicinity.'*

'Can you control the decay of the Bostonians so that we don't accidentally blow ourselves up?' Sally asked.

'Yes. But not well.'

'Can you stop the chain reaction once it has begun?'

'Yes. If I am lucky.'

'If you start such a chain reaction, will the authorities outside know what you're up to?' Sally asked. 'Will they be able to monitor it?'

'Yes.'

'Will it scare them?'

The alien lowered his big head.

'Yes. Very much. You could kill millions of my people.'

Sally smiled at his sad thought. 'Ek, I don't want to kill anybody. I just want to scare your people into giving us back Adam and Watch. But when it is time to bargain, I have to give the impression that I'm a crazy chick from

Spooksville who would just as soon blow up this space station as go swimming in our reservoir at home.'

'What is Spooksville?'

'That's where we come from,' Sally explained. 'And you and your pals are only one of the reasons it has earned that name. You're not even the worst reason. Now broadcast your telepathic message about Adam and Watch and get your Boston bomb ready. Work as fast as you can. I'm still hoping to make it home in time for bed.'

Cindy shook her head doubtfully. 'You're playing with fire, Sally.'

'You don't understand me, Cindy.' Sally rubbed her hands together, excited. 'I'm playing to win.'

Twelve

Hearing the knock on the door, and the telepathic message, Adam and Watch jumped up from their beds and huddled by the door. They could hear nothing outside.

'Who do you think it is?' Adam asked.

'Either Ekwee12 or another alien,' Watch said.

'I know it's either Ekwee12 or another alien. Sally and Cindy haven't become telepathic in the last few hours. The question is, what should we do?'

'If it's someone come to rescue us,' Watch said, 'we'll never forgive ourselves if we don't answer.'

Adam put his mouth close to the door. 'Yeah, we're in here. But who are you?'

The telepathic response was immediate. *'Zhekee191.'*

Adam and Watch looked at each other. 'Their names are kind of corny,' Adam said.

'Imagine if there's hundreds of Zhekees,' Watch agreed.

Adam spoke to the door again. 'What do you want?' he asked.

'Are you two Adam and Watch? The two human beings?'

'Yes,' said Adam. 'How did you learn our names?'

None of the other aliens with the exception of Ekwee12, had asked them.

'Ekwee12 came on our youth network and explained that you two had been taken captive by our government, in violation of our laws. He wanted all of us to fan out and search for you. I know Ekwee12 personally. I am his friend and respect what he says. I know he would not joke about such a serious matter.'

'How were you able to get into this place?'

'My father works here. I have known for many years that we are not encouraged to visit here and it made me wonder if perhaps this was where you had been taken captive. I am pleased to find you so quickly. I have my father's pass key. It allows me to enter and exit this section.'

'Can you open this door?' Adam asked.

'Yes. I just have to push the button beside the door and it will open.'

Again Adam and Watch looked at each other. 'He might have said so at the beginning,' Adam said.

'Perhaps he's afraid how ugly we'll look,' Watch said.

'I know what you look like, of course. I will open the door.'

The door opened right then. Zhekee191 could have been Ekwee12's identical twin brother. He stared up at them with his big black almond-shaped eyes.

'You are tall.'

'We get taller, as time goes on,' Adam said. 'Where is Ekwee12?'

'He did not say specifically but he must still be in the space dock.'

'Do you know if he has our friends, Sally and Cindy, with him?' Watch asked.

'No. He did not mention them in his message. Are they female humans?'

'Yes.' Adam paused. 'How did you guess that?'

'I have studied your culture. It is a required class in our culture.'

'I didn't know we were so important,' Adam said. 'Are you guys planning to invade our planet?'

Zhekee191 seemed taken back.

'We could not do that. It would not be possible.'

'Then how or why do you know so much about us?' Watch asked.

'Because you made us who we are. Of course.'

'Of course,' Adam muttered. He had no idea what the alien was talking about, nor did he really care. He just wanted to get home. He was starving for a real Earth dinner. 'Can you take us to the space dock?' he asked.

'*That is what I wish to do. But we have to be careful. You are not easy to hide. I know a special way there that few take.*'

'Can you get us a weapon?' Watch asked.

'*What do you need a weapon for?*'

'Protection,' Adam said. 'We have already been shot by your people once today. We would not shoot anybody unless we were attacked. You have our word.'

'*I cannot get you a weapon. I do not even know where they are stored.*'

'Take us to the space dock then,' Adam said. 'And thanks in advance for all your help.'

Watch glanced back in the direction of the captured hyeet. 'I hate to leave that hairy guy. I feel like he's almost one of us.'

Adam nodded. 'Maybe we can rescue him later. But right now we have to take care of ourselves.'

They hurried out of the cell and raced down a long hallway. Right away Adam could see they were going a different direction from before. The hallways were similar to the others, but there were differences too. For example, after several hundred metres, they entered a glass hallway that looked out over a massive park area. The green area had to be miles across. It was crowded with thousands of aliens. Some seemed to be playing games, others were just relaxing by small lakes.

Yet there was no sun in the sky. There *was* no real sky, just a wide curving ceiling that glowed with gentle yellow light. Adam wondered if Watch might have been right. Maybe the aliens had polluted their planet so badly that they had to live in space, whether they wanted to or not.

Maybe that was why they kept coming to Earth.

To take it over.

Adam didn't care what Zhekee191 said. He was still worried about invasion.

Adam was glad no one looked up while they were in the glass hallway.

It would have been hard to outrun thousands.

But before they could reach the space dock, they did run into a guard. He appeared to be out looking for them. In his hand he carried a ray-gun and when he saw them he immediately aimed it at them. They received a strong and clear telepathic message.

'*Stop where you are and put your hands over your head.*'

Where they were, fortunately, was half a metre from a corner. Adam and Watch exchanged quick knowing glances. No way were they going back in that cage. They jumped for cover, behind the corner. There was a flash of green light – but it bounced harmlessly off the wall behind them.

Zhekee191 was taken by surprise. He continued to stand in the spot where the guard had spotted them. Watch moved to run away but Adam grabbed his arm and pulled him tight against the wall, right next to the corner.

'Let's take him,' Adam whispered.

The alien security guard had obviously not grown up on spy movies. The guy came running round the corner without any thought that they might be waiting for him. Adam simply stuck out his foot. The guy tripped; he went down hard. In fact, he seemed to knock himself out when his big fat head hit the floor. Adam reached down and grabbed his weapon, which had bounced free. Zhekee191 stared at them with a mixture of wonder and terror.

'*You are an interesting species.*'

'We have our good points,' Adam admitted. He showed Zhekee191 the weapon. 'How do I control the power on this thing?'

It was very simple. If he turned the little knob next to the handle clockwise, the power went up. There were ten settings. *One* stood for light stun. *Two* was hard stun. *Four* and up could kill, Zhekee191 warned. Adam left the weapon on *two*, where it had originally been set. But in his own mind he did not rule out the possibility of increasing the power. One way or another, he vowed, they were taking a space ship to Earth. Zhekee191 was more worried than ever.

'Please do not hurt anyone.'

'We only want to go home,' Adam said.

Zhekee191 led them on their way. Ten minutes later they reached the space dock. There was no transition. One second they were in a narrow hallway; the next they were in the gigantic space harbour. Adam and Watch were stunned to see a crowd of aliens gathered round one seemingly insignificant saucer. The ship floated at the end of a narrow dock. The aliens were bunched up on the dock like a can of sardines. They had several portable instruments with them. They seemed to be trying to measure what was going on inside the ship. The vessel looked exactly like the craft they had taken from Earth to the alien station. But Adam quickly realised that it was the one that held Sally and Cindy, not to mention Ekwee12.

Adam could dimly sense the buzzing thoughts.

The alien crowd was worried.

Adam planned to give them one more thing to worry about. He turned the power on his hand weapon up to *ten* and pointed it at the crowd. He had only been taught the rules of poker a few hours ago but he had learned them well.

'This gun is set to kill!' he shouted. 'Stand aside or I will fire!'

Thirteen

Ekwee12 had broadcast his telepathic network message to search for the humans some time ago. He had also started the Zelithium 110-Hyperzoid-Quartz-Bostonian chain reaction. The growing critical mass was definitely something the alien scientists could sense with their instruments – if the size of the crowd outside was any indication. Sally had already issued her demand for Adam and Watch to be released. She threatened to blow up the space station if they were not. But so far her friends had not been handed over. Sally believed that the chain reaction would have to get closer to the critical point before the aliens would do what she wanted.

But things were happening quickly.

At what Ekwee12 called Level 84 Bostonians, the reactor would blow.

They were now at Level 65.

Ekwee12 did not believe he could stop the reaction after Level 80.

'We're lucky they haven't tried to burn the door down,' Cindy muttered, watching the viewing ports along the wall.

Ekwee12 looked up from the control panel. *'They are afraid we will speed up the reaction if they try.'*

Sally continued to pace. The tension was growing unbearable.

'We're not leaving without them,' Sally muttered.

'I don't get you,' Cindy said. 'One minute you were ready to fly home without them. The next you're ready to sacrifice millions of lives to get them.'

'A girl has a right to change her mind,' Sally said.

'Are your people willing to sacrifice this station to prevent Adam and Watch from escaping?' Cindy asked Ekwee12, feeling desperate.

'I would have said no. My people cherish life. I do not understand why they are being so stubborn.' Ekwee12 glanced at his instruments. *'We have jumped to Level 72.'*

'So quickly?' Cindy asked, shocked.

'The reaction accelerates quickly as it reaches critical mass.'

'How much time do we have?' Sally asked.

'To stop the reaction, maybe three of your minutes. To the explosion, five minutes.'

'We have to back down,' Cindy said.

'We're not backing down!' Sally said. 'A bluff doesn't work unless you push it to the limit!'

'At the reservoir you were bluffing with rocks!' Cindy said. 'That wasn't gambling. *This* is gambling. You're risking our lives.'

'No guts, no glory,' Sally said. Yet she seemed uncertain. She paused in mid-stride, thoughtful. 'Ek, you have not recently checked your computer map of where everyone is supposed to be. Try locating Adam and Watch now.'

'What are you thinking?' Cindy asked.

'Maybe the aliens don't know where Adam and Watch are so they can't hand them over to us.'

'That's impossible,' Cindy said.

'Not if they've escaped,' Sally said.

Once again, Ekwee12 failed to locate Adam and Watch on his computer map. But it didn't matter, anyway. Glancing again out of the viewing ports, Cindy almost had a heart attack.

'There they are!' Cindy screamed. 'It's Adam and Watch!'

Sally pounded her fist in the air. 'I knew the bluff would work!'

'No!' Cindy said quickly. 'The aliens are not handing them over willingly. Adam has a gun. He's pointing it at the crowd. They must have broken free.'

'Just as I suspected,' Sally said. She turned to Ek. 'Open hailing frequencies.'

'What?'

'She wants to talk to the outside,' Cindy explained. 'Is there a way?'

'Yes. Of course.' Ekwee12 pushed a button. '*Speak and they will hear you.*'

'How close are we now?' Sally asked.

'*Level 75. We have less than two minutes to stop the chain reaction.*'

Sally cleared her throat and spoke loudly and formally. 'Adam, Watch – this is Captain Sara Wilcox of the Starship UFO. I am pleased to learn of your escape, and I approve of your resorting to blatant force to fight your way to freedom. But I feel an obligation to inform you that my starship is going to explode in two minutes and that everything for a radius of one thousand miles will be completely destroyed. Over?'

Outside, near the dock, Adam and Watch looked at each other. 'I think the power has gone to her brain,' Watch said.

'Is she bluffing?' Adam asked.

'I hope so,' Watch said. He gestured to the crowd of aliens that separated them from the ship. 'I think she's trying to scare these guys into letting all of us go.'

98

Zhekee191 shifted uneasily beside them.

'She is scaring me. I would be happy to let you go.'

Adam sighed, the gun still in his hand. 'I don't know what to do. I can't really fire this thing. I might hurt someone.'

'Somebody has to back down,' Watch said darkly. 'Or soon none of us will be feeling any pain.'

Inside the ship Ekwee12 informed Sally that they had jumped to Level 78. *'We have less than a minute.'*

'Why don't they let us go?' Sally demanded, getting exasperated. 'Can't they see that I'm serious? Do they want to die?'

'I do not understand them. I do not understand why they kidnapped you in the first place.'

'We must stop the chain reaction!' Cindy cried. 'The bluff has failed!'

'We can't stop!' Sally shouted back. 'If we do we'll never get out of here!'

'We have jumped to Level 79.'

'I would rather be alive here than dead!' Cindy yelled.

'Alive in a cage?' Sally demanded. 'That's no life!'

'I say we stop it!' Cindy shouted. 'And I have as much say as you! Ek, pull the plug!'

'Which plug am I supposed to pull?'

'Wait!' Sally cried.

'Wait for what?' Cindy screamed. 'Death?'

'Do it then!' Sally shouted bitterly, turning away. 'Surrender. That's all you're good for.'

Cindy bent over the control panel beside Ekwee12. 'Stop the reaction. Do it now.'

Ekwee12's four-fingered hands flew over the control panel. Then he sat perfectly still, waiting for some response to the chain reaction. He looked up at her with his big head. His whole body seemed to twitch.

'*It is too late.*'

'What?' Cindy cried.

'*We have jumped to Level 81. Nothing can stop it from exploding.*'

Cindy felt the life go out of her. She glanced over at Sally.

'Well, you got what you wanted,' Cindy said to her back. 'We're doomed.'

For a second, Sally froze, then she suddenly whirled on Ekwee12. 'Can we fly the ship out of space dock?' she asked. 'If we tell them we can't stop it, and they let us go, do we have time to get the ship clear of the station?'

Ekwee12 consulted his instruments.

'*Yes. I can still manoeuvre the ship. If they let us go, we can move it out of the station before the explosion.*'

'Talk to them,' Sally said. 'Send a strong thought,

whatever. Hurry!' Sally put a hand on Cindy's shoulder. 'You get off the ship. I'll ride out with Ek. I got him into this mess. If he has to die, I'll die with him.'

Cindy patted her hand. 'Sally, you amaze me. You're so brave.'

Ekwee12 jumped up quickly. *'They have opened the outside station doors for us. I have programmed the ship to fly into deep space. None of us has to stay here. None of us has to die.'*

'Actually,' Sally admitted, with a faint smile, 'I was hoping he was going to say that.'

The saucer door opened. They jumped out on to the dock. They were hardly clear of the ship when it took off at high speed behind them. They caught a flash of it going through the huge dark entrance – then it was gone. A minute passed while aliens and humans alike held their breath. Sally and Cindy waited for a huge shock wave, but none came. Then a wave of relief rippled through the gathering. Beside them, Ekwee12 calmly informed them that the ship had exploded safely out of the way.

'But we didn't feel anything!' Sally said. 'Was it a huge explosion.'

'Yes. But the ship is fast. It took place far from here, and there is no shock wave in space. You would not feel anything unless we were being destroyed.'

101

Sally nodded wearily. 'Well, it's done then. We're caught.'

The crowd parted so the four humans could at least be together. Adam surrendered his gun. There seemed no point in keeping it after a nuclear bomb had failed to move the aliens to release them. The guys patted the girls on their backs.

'Thank you for coming for us,' Adam said.

'That was an awesome bluff,' Watch agreed. 'I would have fallen for it.'

Sally shook her head. 'Not you. You're too cool a player.'

Watched glanced at Adam. 'I'm not saying anything,' Adam said.

There was nothing to say. Alien guards grabbed hold of their arms. The crude message was clear. They were going to be taken to the cages. Ekwee12 and Zhekee191 tried to protest, but they were pulled aside by the government authorities. Adam wondered what their punishment would be. He felt almost as bad for them as he did for himself and his friends. And they had come so close to escaping. It made the final defeat that much more bitter.

Yet all was not lost.

Suddenly, all around the circular space port, on maybe fifty different levels, young aliens poured into view. There were dozens at first, then hundreds. Within a couple of minutes, as Adam and his friends stood spellbound, the number swelled to at least two thousand. None of the aliens were over half a metre tall, but their combined telepathic message was very clear, and very powerful.

'LET THE HUMANS GO! THEY HAVE DONE US NO HARM!'

Ekwee12 broke free of the authorities and hurried to their side.

His thoughts were excited. *'These are my friends on the network. They are not going to let this injustice continue. They are demanding your release.'*

Adam laughed. 'Even us dull humans are able to pick up that kind of mental message. The question is, will your authorities do what your kids say?'

'I think they will have to. In our culture, kids are allowed to vote.'

'Cool,' Sally said. 'If that was true in our culture, I would be president.'

Another few minutes went by. The alien authorities huddled. The alien guards continued to hold on to the humans. But as time passed, more kids flooded the area. The huddled aliens seemed to grow even more uneasy. The young aliens' mental voice was like a huge washing wave of reason that could not be ignored. Finally a tall alien dressed in a gold suit took Ekwee12 aside. They conferred for a minute or two, then Ekwee12 ran to their side. He took Adam and Sally's hands and looked up at them with his big black eyes. Once again, he tried to smile. It was a good effort; this time there was real joy in the expression. *'They are letting you go. They have told me to take you home.'*

Fourteen

Far out in space, close to the hyperjump, Sally said that Cindy had said that Adam looked like Ekwee12. Adam was taken aback; he felt insulted.

'I don't believe Cindy said any such thing,' Adam replied.

'She did,' Sally said. 'Just ask her.'

Adam looked at Cindy. 'Well?'

Cindy hesitated. 'I said Ek *reminded* me of you. I didn't say you looked alike.'

'How do I remind you of an alien?' Adam wanted to know.

Ekwee12 spoke from his place at the control panel. *'We are both cute.'*

'That's it, exactly,' Cindy said with a smile.

Adam had to laugh. 'I suppose I've been called worse.'

'It makes me feel sick that he is flattered even by her insults,' Sally said to Watch.

'You're the captain,' Watch said. 'Why don't you have them both thrown overboard?'

'I've already gone to too much trouble to save them,' Sally muttered.

Ekwee12 turned and looked at them. '*We are almost up to the jump. I was wondering what precise time you would like to be returned?*'

That made them all sit up.

'Can this ship travel in time?' Watch said.

'*Of course. You travelled in time on the journey here. Did you not know that?*'

'How could we know?' Adam said. 'We thought this was just a regular space ship.'

'*But you saw how much Earth had changed. You must have known we had jumped forward in time.*'

They all stared at each other, shocked.

'Do you mean that you are from Earth?' Adam asked, barely able to get the words out. 'In the future?'

'*Yes. I thought you knew.*'

Sally was disgusted. 'But you're fat-headed . . . you're such an unusual alien shape. I don't understand.'

'*I am not an alien. I told you.*'

'But where have all the people on Earth gone?' Sally asked. 'Did you invade and wipe them all out?'

Ekwee12 shook his head. He must have picked up this

106

gesture from being with them. *'We are the people of Earth. We are what you will change into after another two hundred thousand years of evolution.'*

Sally was indignant. 'No way. My great-great-great-grandchildren are not going to look like you. I won't have it.'

'I think you need another two thousand "greats" in front of "grandchildren" to match the time frame he's talking about,' Watch said.

'If we do become you,' Adam said, 'why do you live in space?'

Ekwee12 lowered his head. *'You, we – we dirtied our planet. We cannot live there any more.'*

'But now that we know that,' Adam said hopefully, 'maybe we can work to stop people from polluting the Earth so much. I know I will try, as soon as I grow up and get out of Spooksville and get a real life.'

Ekwee12 raised his head. Once more he tried to smile. *'That could help us all.'*

'I don't know if I accept this,' Sally said. 'But for the sake of argument, say you *are* a more advanced form of us. Why would your people go into the past to steal us? For what purpose?'

'I meant to tell you this. When I conferred with our highest government official, he apologised and said that the government

had wanted a few kids from your generation to study to see how to liven up our culture. Lately we have become somewhat stagnant as a race.'

Sally laughed. 'He got more than he bargained for.'

'That is precisely what he conveyed to me. He thought we needed kids from an earlier, more calm generation. You guys were too explosive. But in either case, he promised that anyone else we took from the past would not be kidnapped. They could come with us only if they wanted to.'

'Can you see about getting that hyeet freed?' Watch said. 'He was in the cage across from us. He looked pretty miserable.'

'Now that we know the truth, the youth of our culture will demand that no intelligent creature is kept hostage. It should not have happened to begin with.'

'I agree with that,' Cindy said. 'This has been a long day.'

'That is what I am asking you. I can return you home at any time you wish. You have only to tell me when.'

'We should probably return just after we were kidnapped,' Adam suggested. 'After both ships left. I don't want to go running into myself.'

'I agree,' Watch said.

'Sounds good,' Sally said. 'That way we can make it home in time for dinner.'

But Cindy suddenly jumped up. 'We have to land before we left. We have to come in unobserved, and put down on the hill near the Haunted Cave.'

'Why?' they all asked.

Cindy was thoughtful. 'It's hard to explain. Just trust me on this one. Ek, do you have a ray-gun aboard this ship?'

'Yes. Why?'

'I will need to borrow it just after we land. Put us down just before the other two ships appeared. But like I said, don't let anyone – including ourselves – see us.'

'Cindy,' Adam warned, 'we don't want to tamper with time. Let our earlier versions have the adventure. It was fun, and it turned out all right in the end.'

But Cindy was adamant. 'No. This way is the only way. You'll see why when we get there.'

Cindy refused to change her mind, so they instructed Ekwee12 to do as she said. Ekwee12 adjusted the hyper-jump so that they burst through to their time a few hours early. In fact, he gave them enough leeway that they were able to swing by Jupiter, Saturn and Mars and have a look. Watch said the planets were much more impressive up close than in his telescope.

'I'm going to have to get one of these saucers,' he said with a sigh.

Finally, they landed on the hill near the Haunted Cave. Ekwee12 turned off the saucer's lights. They came down unobserved, then jumped out of the ship. It was still warm but it was good to be back, and feel normal earth beneath them. Even if they were in Spooksville once more, home was home.

Far below, they could see themselves sitting by the reservoir.

Cindy was still soaking her foot in the water.

'Oh,' said Cindy, wincing as she put her foot down. 'You guys will have to help me down the ravine. Ekwee12, I need that gun.'

'Are you injured, Cindy?'

'Yes. I sprained my ankle before you guys showed up.'

'Why didn't you tell me? I have something that will fix that.'

Ekwee12 disappeared inside. When he returned he carried a ray-gun and a small silver ball. Instructing Cindy to sit down, he placed the ball near her ankle. The ball began to glow a dull red colour. After a couple of minutes, Cindy let out a soft cry of delight. She flexed her foot and Ekwee12 withdrew the strange instrument.

'My ankle's all better! How did you do that, Ek?'

'We know a lot more about human, and alien, bodies in our time.'

'Great.' Cindy jumped up and grabbed the weapon. 'I have a job I have to take care of. The first setting is stun, right Ek?'

'That is correct.'

'Who are you going to stun?' Adam insisted.

'You'll see,' Cindy said. 'You guys can come with me if you're very quiet.'

Together, Ekwee12 included, they crept further down the hill, until they were almost able to hear the earlier version of themselves talking. No surprise, two alien ships suddenly appeared in the sky. They watched everything that had happened before, up until Watch was taken inside the first saucer. Then Cindy said they had to move closer.

'We shouldn't interfere,' Sally repeated.

'We won't,' Cindy promised. 'Everything will be just as it was.'

They crept cautiously around until they were at the lip of the ravine. Down below, the fighting started. Adam and Sally were stunned by the alien weapons. But back up on the hill, to everyone's surprise – except Cindy's – two aliens walked by just below them. To their even greater surprise they saw an earlier version of Cindy stand up on the opposite side of the ravine. She had a big rock in her hands.

Her intention was clear. She was going to brain one or

both of the aliens. They watched in amazement as she raised the rock above her head and threw it down. At that exact instant, *their* Cindy whipped out her gun and aimed and fired. There was a flash of green light. She stunned the aliens, and the two collapsed in a pile. The rock had missed by a mile. Cindy laughed quietly beside them in the dark as her earlier version peered confused over the edge of the ravine.

'I wondered why those guys just fell over on me,' she whispered.

Epilogue

It was time to say goodbye to Ekwee12. They hated to see him leave.

'Why don't you hang out with us for a while?' Adam asked. 'There's always a lot happening here. Things are never stagnant.'

'Yeah, you can learn a lot from us about how awesome kids are in this century,' Sally said.

I would love to stay. But I have work to do at home cleaning up the confusion caused by your illegal capture. I have to return and make sure it never happens again.

'But when you've finished your job, stop by some time,' Cindy pleaded. 'We like you. You're one of us.'

Ekwee12 held out his hands for each of them to touch. *You will see me again, I promise.*

They said their goodbyes. Cindy had a tear in her eye. Maybe they all did. But just as Ekwee12 was about to disappear inside his ship, Sally called one last question.

'Hey, Ek?' she said. 'Do you know why it is so hot here these days? We never have weather like this.'

'*A heavy inversion layer has settled over this portion of your coast. It will clear up in a couple of days and then you will have cooler temperatures.*'

'It's not a witch's curse, after all,' Adam teased her.

Sally nodded, insulted. 'I knew that.'

If you've enjoyed *Aliens in the Sky*, turn the page for the first chapter in Christopher Pike's next Spooksville chiller . . .

The Cold People

One

It was another Spooksville mystery.

The town was freezing, and it was still summer. The cold weather was as strange as the boiling temperatures had been a couple of weeks earlier when Adam and his friends had run into the aliens. None of them could understand what had brought on the chilly snap. That Monday morning, when they'd got up, every window in town was coated with a fine layer of white frost. Little did they know that, by the time the sun went down, there would be frost *inside* many of the people who lived in Spooksville.

Adam, Sally, Watch and Cindy started off the day by having their usual milk and doughnuts at the local bakery. Because of the cold, they each had a cup of coffee with their breakfast as well, just to warm their bones. To their surprise, Watch had a thermometer in one of the four watches he regularly wore. He studied it as they munched their food. He doubted the temperature would get above freezing all day.

'It's still in the low twenties,' he said. 'If we're going to be outside today, we better keep moving.'

They took Watch's suggestion to heart, and decided to spend the day hiking in the woods in the hills behind Spooksville. They pedalled their bikes most of the way there, hiding them in a cluster of trees when the road ran out. Adam had been up in the hills before, of course, when he had visited the Haunted Cave and the reservoir, but he had never been to the wooded area. He was amazed at the size and varieties of the trees.

'This wood looks like something out of *Hansel and Gretel*,' he said as they hiked along a narrow dirt path covered with pine needles. He wore a heavy jacket but unzipped it as he walked. The exercise was taking away some of the chill.

Sally snorted. 'Hansel and Gretel were lightweights. They only had one old witch to kill and it made them famous. We get worse than that every week and no one writes about us.'

'We need a press agent,' Watch agreed. 'Our life stories need to be on TV.'

'Personally I like being unknown,' Cindy said. 'I

117

don't need all the money and fame.'

'Wait till you're a few years older,' Sally said. 'Money and fame will be what you crave the most.'

'I think all that stuff is superficial,' Cindy shrugged.

Sally sniggered. 'Spoken like a true liberal. In this world you've got to cash in when you can. For that reason I've started to keep a journal of my experiences. If I don't die in the next ten years, I figure I'll be able to auction the movie rights to my life.'

'Am I in your journal?' Adam asked.

Sally hesitated. 'You're mentioned in a small footnote.'

It was Cindy's turn to snigger. 'I bet the whole journal is about Adam.'

'That's not true,' Sally said quickly.

'Ha,' Cindy said. 'Prove it: let us read it.'

'You can read it,' Sally said. 'In exchange for a million bucks.'

As usual, Sally had the last word. They continued up the path without further conversation. Soon it began to narrow as the trees grew thicker. It could have been close to dark, the way the heavy branches hung over them. The shade was that deep. Yet Adam could still see his breath as he exhaled. Once again he wondered at the strange weather and what could be causing it. He knew there must be a reason.

They were almost finished exploring and about to turn back when they spotted them: the Cold People. Adam saw them first, but initially he just thought they were huge blocks of ice jammed inbetween the trees. That in itself would have been strange enough, but there was something even weirder: though there was frost in the surrounding branches, there was no actual snow. For that matter, the sun was still out, there were no clouds in the sky.

'Hey,' Adam said, pointing to a spot fifteen metres off the path. 'What's that?'

They all peered in the shadows.

'Looks like a glacier,' Sally said.

'The ice age would have to arrive for us to have a glacier here,' Cindy said.

'This town is not known for standard weather patterns,' Sally said. 'Two winters ago we had an iceberg float into our harbour. It stayed offshore for a couple of months. We had incredible snowball fights, until this polar bear came out of a hidden cave and ate Buddy Silverstone.'

Cindy snorted. 'I don't believe it.'

'There actually was an iceberg,' Watch said. 'But it was an Eskimo who came out of the cave. And he just invited Buddy to dinner.'

'Yeah, but he didn't tell Buddy that he was the main course,' Sally said.

'Would you guys stop arguing and tell me what we're looking at,' Adam said.

Cindy squinted. 'Looks like big blocks of ice.'

'We know that,' Sally said impatiently. 'But what is the nature of these blocks of ice? Are they composed of frozen water? Are they from this planet? You have to ask yourself these questions.'

'Why don't we take a closer look,' Watch suggested.

It was a reasonable idea, although it was harder to get to the ice blocks than Adam had imagined. The trees were so compact in this part of the woods – Adam felt as if they would squeeze him to a pulp (no pun intended). But he told himself he was overreacting because of his first day in Spooksville when a tree had tried to eat him alive. And he had thought *that* was a strange day. Looking back, it had been pretty normal for this town.

There weren't just the two or three blocks of ice as they had first seen from the path, but literally dozens of them. Some were lying down, others stood jammed between the tree trunks. They were almost all identical in size, two metres long by half a metre deep and half a metre wide. Adam and his friends knelt by the first one they came to. It lay flat on its back – and Watch tried to brush off the covering frost. But the block was only vaguely translucent; they could not see into the centre of it.

Yet there was something in there.

Something large and dark.

'These are like frozen coffins,' Sally said softly.

'Where did they come from?' Cindy whispered, fear in her voice. Up close, the ice blocks were sort of scary. Watch continued to brush the covering frost, hoping to come to more transparent ice.

'I don't think the ice-cream man put them here,' Sally said.

'This block is really cold,' Watch said, pausing to breathe on his unprotected hand. 'And I don't mean that it's ice cold.'

'What do you mean?' Cindy asked.

'Let me show you,' Watch said. He took off his watch that held the thermometer and laid it on top of the block. He left it there for perhaps ten seconds before he snapped it back up. He studied the reading. 'Ten degrees Fahrenheit,' he muttered.

'That's twelve degrees below freezing,' Sally whispered, amazed.

'That's a lot colder than the air temperature,' Adam said.

Watch nodded. 'Unless these blocks were just dropped here a few minutes ago – which I doubt – something inside them is generating incredible cold.' He tapped at the block with the knuckles on his right hand, then leaned over and sniffed it. 'I don't even think this is frozen water.'

'What is it then?' Cindy asked.

Watch frowned. 'It has a faint ammonia smell. But it's not ammonia.' He glanced at Adam. 'I would like to thaw one of these.'

'Do you think that's a good idea?' Adam asked.

'No,' Sally and Cindy said quickly together. They glanced at each other in surprise. It was seldom they agreed upon anything.

Sally continued, 'There may be something inside we don't want to thaw.'

'Like what?' Adam asked.

Sally shook her head darkly. 'You know this town. We could have anything from a bloodthirsty vampire to a blob from Planet Zeon inside here. I have a personal rule against fooling with strange artefacts that might end up eating me.'

'That rule must make your journal pretty boring,' Cindy remarked.

'There is a coincidence here that we're forgetting,' Adam said. 'It is freezing today and it's still summer. These blocks are colder than freezing. Is it possible there is a connection between the two?'

122

Watch nodded. 'You make a good point. But I can say for a fact that these blocks alone are not cooling off this entire area.'

'I'm not saying that,' Adam replied. 'I mean that these blocks may have arrived here today because it is cold.'

'You mean whoever put them here might be behind the cold?' Cindy asked.

'Exactly,' Adam said.

'I think we have to take the risk,' Watch said. 'We have to thaw one. It's possible that there's nothing inside.'

'I have my Bic lighter,' Sally said reluctantly. 'We could gather some dry sticks and build a fire beside it.'

'But the fire might hurt whatever is inside the block,' Cindy said.

'Personally I'm not worried about that,' Sally said.

'If we're careful with the flames,' Watch said. 'I'm sure we can avoid damaging the contents of the block.'

Adam nodded. 'I do think we have to have a look at what's inside. I know I won't be able to sleep wondering about it. As long as we all know that once we have thawed whatever this is, we probably won't be able to freeze it again.'

Sally agreed. 'This is like opening Pandora's Box. There'll be no turning back.'

Exclusive watch for
Spooksville
fans!

Even Watch would be pleased to add this fantastic bubble watch to his collection! It's a digital time keeper with a difference! For one thing there's a special Spooksville bat floating around inside!

The watch is totally exclusive and can be yours for only £4.99 (incl. post and packing).

TAKE ADVANTAGE OF THIS SPECIAL OFFER. COLLECT SIX SPECIAL TOKENS AND CLAIM THE WATCH ABSOLUTELY FREE. COLLECT THREE TOKENS AND GET THE WATCH FOR ONLY £2.50

You'll find the tokens in special editions of Spooksville. Look for the flash on the cover

---